Praise for Kimberly Van Meter

"[Kimberly] Van Meter, a new Harlequin Blaze author, comes out swinging with a rekindled love story."
—*RT Book Reviews* on *The Hottest Ticket in Town*

"Talk about *heat*! Ms. Van Meter should give out fire extinguishers with the story."
—*Harlequin Junkie* on *The Hottest Ticket in Town*

Praise for Liz Talley

"[Liz] Talley uses her skill to create authentic characters whose emotions and activities ring true."
—*RT Book Reviews* on *The Sweetest September*

"Sexy characters and an interesting plotline make Talley's tale a must read."
—*RT Book Reviews* on *His Uptown Girl*

Kimberly Van Meter wrote her first book at sixteen and finally achieved publication in December 2006. She writes for the Harlequin Superromance, Blaze and Romantic Suspense lines. She and her husband of seventeen years have three children, three cats and always a houseful of friends, family and fun.

Liz Talley, a 2009 Golden Heart Award finalist in Regency romance, has since found a home writing sassy Southern stories. Her book *Vegas Two-Step* debuted in June 2010 and was quickly followed by four more books in her Oak Stand, Texas, series. In her current books, she's visiting her home state of Louisiana. Liz lives in north Louisiana with her hero, two beautiful boys and a passel of animals. She enjoys laundry, paying bills and creating masterful dinners for her family. She also lies in her biography to make herself look like the perfect housewife. What she really likes is new shoes, lemon-drop martinis and fishing off the pier at her camp. You can visit her at liztalleybooks.com to learn more about the lies she tells herself and about her upcoming books.

To get the inside scoop on Harlequin Blaze and its talented writers, be sure to check out BlazeAuthors.com.

All backlist available in ebook format.

Visit the Author Profile page at Harlequin.com for more titles.

Kimberly Van Meter
Liz Talley

A Wrong Bed Christmas

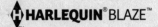

ISBN-13: 978-0-373-79873-5

A Wrong Bed Christmas
Copyright © 2015 by Harlequin Books S.A.

The publisher acknowledges the copyright holders of the individual works as follows:

Ignited
Copyright © 2015 by Kimberly Van Meter

Where There's Smoke
Copyright © 2015 by Liz Talley

PLEASE RECYCLE
THIS PRODUCT IS RECYCLABLE

Recycling programs for this product may not exist in your area.

Printed in U.S.A.

HARLEQUIN®
www.Harlequin.com

CONTENTS

Dear Reader,

When I was asked if I would like to participate in a sexy Christmastime anthology with one of my favorite former Superromance authors, Liz Talley, my answer was an immediate and enthusiastic yes! And I'm so happy I did.

New characters, new settings and the chance to work side by side with an author I truly respect and admire isn't work—it's pure joy. If only everyone were this lucky, right?

And there's just something to be said for the holidays. Everyone is happier, the lights are twinkly and sometimes clothes are just a bother.

Here's hoping this sexy anthology warms up those frosty nights when you're waiting for Santa to bring you something nice...or naughty!

Warmly,

Kimberly Van Meter

IGNITED

Kimberly Van Meter

1

ALEXIS MATHESON WAS dreaming of Christmas cookies and homemade candies and stressing over how her candy thermometer was not working properly—when the scenario changed abruptly.

Suddenly, she was wrapped in a shadow lover's arms, enjoying a sizzling kiss that was hotter than baking peanut brittle and she hazily wondered who her dream lover was and why she was torturing herself with a sex dream when she'd sternly declared a moratorium on sex until she got her head on straight.

Ugh. Plainly her brain thought that might take forever.

Ah, dream lover was pretty good with his tongue and hands! Now, why had she determined sex was a bad idea for the time being?

She moaned, wrapping her arms around her lover, sighing with pleasure as his mouth blazed a trail down the column of her neck, nipping and nibbling and sending goose bumps tripping down her skin.

Everything felt so real and yet dreamy at the same

time. Hell, if dream lovers were this entertaining, maybe she could give up wide-awake sex for good.

Ha! Very funny.

She groaned again as a strong hand found her breast and squeezed and suddenly her eyes fluttered open at the realization that something didn't feel right—no, it felt fabulous, but that's not what she meant—she no longer knew if what was happening was only in her mind.

Before her sleep-fuzzed brain could fully react, she was being kissed again and, damn, it was good.

But wait a minute…she'd gone to bed alone!

An instant shot of adrenaline chased away her sleepy enjoyment of Mr. Talented Stranger and replaced it with a holy-shit-I'm-about-to-become-a-statistic jolt of awareness and she shoved at the big body covering her, landing a strategic hit to his groin area as she kicked.

He grunted in pain and rolled to his side, doubled over.

Every serial-killer book and movie she'd ever happened to read or see jumped to mind as she used her feet to shove the stranger's massive body right off the edge of her bed and onto the floor.

"This bed is already *occupado*!"

Once she heard the thump of his body landing on her carpet, she sprang from the bed and flicked on the light, snatching the first thing she could grab, and hurled it at the stranger when he stumbled to his feet. *Oh, good Lord, he was naked.*

He dodged the shoe, yelling, "What are you doing? Stop throwing shit! You've already mashed my nuts, lady!" as he shielded his frank and beans and blinked against the light like a mole squinting at the sun. "Watch it!"

"No, *you* watch it, this is my room and, more important, my bed. You have ten seconds to tell me who you are before you get a Martha Stewart smackdown." She hefted the book in her hands with the smiling domestic goddess gracing the hardcover to show she meant business, but the sturdy, dark-haired guy looked strong enough to take a hit without breaking a sweat. Even under the circumstances, Alexis would've had to have been blind to miss the fact that her intruder had a body that was worth taking a second look at. Go figure. A sexy intruder. Why did she have the worst luck with men?

"Calm down," he grumbled. "Put the damn book down, you crazy lunatic."

"Wrong answer," Alexis retorted and heaved the book straight at his head.

He tried to evade the projectile, but it caught him on the shoulder. "Holy hell! That hurt!" he yelled and then snatched up his jeans and jerked them on even as he stumbled/ran from her room, but not before she caught a quick glimpse of a near-perfect ass. *What a tragedy*, she thought before leaping after him, determined to find out who'd had the gall to climb into her bed, but her foot caught on her suitcase and she went hard to the floor, twisting her ankle in the process.

She'd once been accused of having an obsessive type of laser focus when it suited her, which was why instead of babying her foot, she continued to run after the stranger with the hot ass as he skidded into her brother, Erik's, room.

"Your sister's crazy, man," the guy said, glowering in Alexis's direction just as Alexis realized that Erik was home and she'd offered her best friend, Emma, her brother's bed. *Oh crud.* Stopping short, Alexis registered confusion all around, which under different circumstances might've been funny as hell, but there was nothing funny about the way her ankle was beginning to throb.

"What the hell, Erik? Who *is* this?" she asked, wincing as her abused ankle started to really protest. What the hell had she done to her foot?

Alexis shot a brief, apologetic look to Emma who was watching the situation unfold with wide eyes, the blankets tucked tightly beneath her arms as if trying to superglue the cloth to her body. *Egad. Poor Emma.* Alexis was going to have to bake an extra batch of lemon bars for this little snafu.

Erik, ever the peacemaker, stepped between Alexis and the man scowling hard enough to freeze his face that way, trying to be the voice of reason in this awkward situation. "Hey, hey," he said when Alexis didn't immediately back down.

"Jesus, woman," the man beside Erik said to Alexis, still miffed that she'd tried to neuter him with a donkey kick to the jewels. "I didn't know you were in there. Give me a freakin' break."

"What are you still doing here?" Erik said, gently pushing Alexis back to protect his friend.

Alexis stepped back and winced as a jolt of fresh pain took her breath away. "Ow," she gasped, immediately lifting her foot to relieve the pressure. "I think I hurt my ankle," she admitted with an irritated glower when Erik frowned with concern. "And we're here because my memory sucks. I drove to pick up Em, but we decided to take her SUV from her place. Then just as we headed down I-25, I realized I left my laptop charger and we swung back because there wasn't going to be time to get a new one once we got to Emma's parents' place. By the time we could leave again, they had closed parts of the interstate. We figured we'd wait until midmorning to leave. Roads should be clear then."

"So that's why your car wasn't in the driveway," Erik surmised.

"Yeah. I thought you were working," Alexis huffed, moving past Erik to sit on the bed next to Emma so she could get a better look at her ankle.

It was then that Emma whispered, "Lex, you don't have any pants on."

Oh yeah, there was that. She hadn't exactly been planning to entertain and most times she slept naked, so the fact that she had a shirt and underwear on was a bonus. She shrugged, more interested in the state of her ankle than anything else at the moment. "How different is this from my bathing suit? Crap, my ankle is really swelling," she muttered, momentarily forgetting about the guy, her brother and the whole shebang because *holy hell, that smarts!*

But apparently someone else was still holding a grudge because Stranger with the Sexy Ass piped in with, "She punched me and then threw a shoe at me."

"You scared the crap out of me," Alexis said with

a glare. As if he had any room to bitch—if he hadn't been in her bed, she wouldn't have had to defend herself. And she wasn't even going to mention how Grabby McGrabbyhands had been all over her—she wasn't in the mood to clean up a massacre. As even-headed as Erik was, he might take exception to the fact that his friend had been touchy-feely in his supposed sleep.

"Okay, okay." Erik held his hands up, obviously bone tired and not in the mood to deal with this nonsense all night. "Let's all just calm down. This was a big misunderstanding. No harm, no foul."

But Alexis was feeling more petulant by the moment as her ankle ramped up in pain. "Speak for yourself," Alexis muttered, rubbing her ankle. "I tripped over my suitcase when I was chasing that pervert out of my room."

"Pervert?" the guy said. "I'm not a—"

Erik looked aggrieved and shook his head. "He's not a pervert. Well, not usually. This is Layton Davis," Erik said by way of introduction. "He drove me home after we worked a blaze. I told him to take the spare room. I thought you were gone. You were supposed to be gone."

Oh sure, blame it on Alexis's inability to keep details straight. She shot a withering look Layton's way. Was she being irrational? Possibly. Sure, they could chalk it all up to a weird, unfortunate coincidence that would make really funny sitcom fodder, but pain made Alexis ill-tempered and she'd never been much of a good sport when it came to being on the losing end of an argument.

"Well, we weren't gone," Alexis said, unable to keep the grumpiness from her tone. "And who doesn't check where he's going to sleep before plopping down on top of someone?"

"Someone who's tired as shit and unaware someone's friend's sister is occupying the bed he was given," Layton said, clearly just as annoyed and as ready to put the argument to bed as she was.

Erik shrugged, rubbing his eyes. "Like I knew. Let's shelve the accusations and take a page from Emma's book and not freak out."

Everyone looked at Emma. *Oops.* Alexis had forgotten about Emma again. Emma managed an awkward smile and Alexis wanted to say, *I feel ya, sister—this bites,* but didn't because she didn't want to embarrass Emma any more than she already had. And Alexis held no illusions that Emma wasn't mortified to her dainty toes over this mishap. Of the two, Emma was the more reserved, more conservative and least likely to be voted Most Outrageous in a peer poll.

Awkward silence followed as they each came to the conclusion that no further beating could be done on this particular horse and it was time to lay it to rest.

"Okay, good. Now, since it's cold as frick outside and the roads are too dangerous, let's bunk up and get through the night," Erik said.

"Your sister probably needs an ice pack or something," Layton said with a reluctant sigh as if he hated to be helpful in this regard because he was still holding a grudge, and gestured to Alexis's swollen ankle. "How about I grab some ice while you figure out the sleeping arrangements."

It was on the tip of her tongue to tell him not to worry about it, that she could tend to her own injuries, but Layton had already split. Maybe he needed ice for his nuts, too.

It was then that she realized her brother was swaddled in a blanket like a Scottish laird.

"Why are you wearing a quilt?" Alexis asked.

"'Cause I'm naked under here," he said, tugging the quilt up higher.

Ah. *Yeah, good idea.* Therapy for getting an eyeful of her brother's junk was not in her budget. But wait a minute…if he was naked under there…her gaze swung to her friend.

"Wait, did you climb into bed with Emma while you were naked?" Alexis asked, grossed out for Emma. Not that Erik wasn't good-looking, but, *eww,* Erik was like a big brother to Emma, too. He used to torment Emma just as enthusiastically as he'd tormented Alexis. He'd been an equal-opportunity torturer.

"Yeah," Erik admitted, and color climbed Emma's cheeks. Was Emma embarrassed because she'd seen Erik in his birthday suit or, worse, because she'd liked what she'd seen? *Ugh.* The very idea… Alexis couldn't handle it.

"Well, how come you didn't scream?"

"I rarely scream," Emma said, as if that made perfect sense.

"Well, if a big bozo sat on you, you would," Alexis countered, not quite buying Emma's explanation.

But there wasn't time to push the argument because Layton reappeared with a bag of frozen broccoli wrapped in a dish towel. "Here. I'm happy to take the couch," he said.

"And I'll give you your bed back and sleep with Alexis," Emma said to Erik. "I feel so bad about being here when you—"

"I told you to,' Alexis interrupted, still thinking about Emma's reaction. "He was at work."

A beat of awkward silence made ten times weirder because of the questions popping around in Alexis's head followed, until finally, Emma said, "I'm not exactly dressed. And neither is Erik. So..."

"Right," Alexis said, grabbing the frozen-broccoli bag and sliding from the bed, only to gasp at the sudden and unforgiving pain. Erik started as if he wanted to help her but couldn't without dropping the quilt and risking a full-frontal show.

"Well, hell," Layton said with a low grumble before sweeping Alexis into his arms.

"Hey! Put me down," Alexis said, mortified that a) he'd picked her up as if she weighed nothing and b) there was no mistaking the delightfully solid muscle lifting up her backside.

"I will. In your room." Layton strode to the door, ignoring her protests. Alexis shot Emma a pleading glance— as if her friend was going to jump to her rescue when all Layton was doing was being mildly chivalrous—and suffered the knowledge that she was just going to have to suck it up and deal with the fact that this situation couldn't get any more uncomfortable.

But then Alexis knew full well that tempting fate with a thought like that never ended well.

2

LAYTON WAS TIRED, grumpy and his balls ached, but he had to admit that in spite of the fact that Alexis was a firecracker with a short fuse, she felt pretty good in his arms.

And that thought right there was why it was apparent that he wasn't right in the head.

"For what it's worth, I'm sorry about…uh, you know."

Eloquent. He nearly bit his tongue in half with embarrassment at his bumbling apology, but was there a more suave way to apologize for sleep-sexin' someone up?

"All I'm saying is that I'm not that kind of guy," he added gruffly.

Alexis seemed to accept that he was being truthful and nodded, though her cheeks brightened a bit. "Sure. Honest mistake, I guess."

"Yeah."

Layton set her gently on the bed and started to leave, but Alexis stopped him, saying, "Um, so, yeah, sorry about your balls. Self-defense 101, take out the jewels."

"Effective. It'll be a miracle if I can have kids."

She bit her lip around a smile when she realized he was kidding.

Layton exited the bedroom just as Emma was entering. Emma shot Layton a quick look and then joined Alexis on the bed.

"Well, that was eventful," Alexis said with an embarrassed laugh to break the ice. "I bet that was hecka awkward with Erik. Sorry about that. Are you traumatized for life?"

"It's okay," Emma murmured, but there was a subtle flush to her cheeks that made Alexis wonder if Emma had enjoyed the view. Okay, so if Alexis were being objective, her brother was pretty decent to look at, so she supposed it wouldn't be far-fetched to imagine Emma liking what she saw. But Alexis couldn't go there. Emma was her best friend since grade school. Erik had pulled Emma's pigtails and made fun of her braces. Alexis shuddered. "Let's chalk this night up to one unfortunate incident and try to forget about it. Tomorrow, we'll hit the road as soon as the roads are clear. Sound good?"

"Mmm-hmm." Emma climbed into the bed and was already snuggling up to the pillow, all too ready to return to dreamland.

But it wasn't that easy for Alexis. Her adrenaline was still pumping and, worse, the memory of those heated dream kisses that turned out to be real, after all, was making her restless.

She should've known that something was off when

she'd been so incredibly aroused in her dream. No dream was that good.

Not even if chocolate was involved.

She liked to think of herself as relatively smart—she was, after all, in the master's program for her business degree—but if one looked at her track record with relationships, she might not appear to be so intelligent.

Which was why she'd made a vow to herself that until she finished school she was not going to even *think* about guys. Boys, as her dad used to warn her, were bad news.

Except her brother, of course; Erik was a doll.

But all other boys…were persona non grata.

A small sigh escaped her lips. Goodbye fun times, hello celibacy.

It wasn't for forever—just until she got her act together and on track.

So why did it feel like a death sentence?

LAYTON RUBBED THE sore spot on his dome and tried to ignore the dull, throbbing ache from where the book had connected with his shoulder, not to mention the residual sore spot from where Alexis had abused his groin.

Erik had mentioned his younger sister was living with him for the time being while she finished her master's degree, but he hadn't mentioned anything about the woman being a live wire.

Erik also hadn't mentioned anything about how gorgeous his sister was.

That part shouldn't matter, he reminded his randy self as he closed his eyes against the pain. Sexy and crazy were a bad combination—like pickles and eggs on a peanut butter sandwich or Tabasco sauce on chocolate. All sorts of bad and bound to give you indigestion.

But even as he knew it was better to just go to sleep and forget all about Alexis Matheson…how was he supposed to forget the memory of that hot woman writhing in his arms, her mouth on his? Guilt nudged at him. If Erik knew where Layton's mouth had been, Layton would have more than an aching dome to contend with. But damn, if she'd been that hot asleep, what was she like when she was awake?

Those kinds of thoughts were not helpful, he told himself.

Neither was the fact that when she'd leaped from the bed wearing next to nothing, he'd gotten an eyeful of rounded, feminine hips and a rack that wouldn't quit. A nice, generous handful for sure. And that thin silky chemise hadn't given much coverage. He was pretty sure he'd caught a tantalizing view of her breasts—and what his eyes had only caught a glimpse of, his hands had touched, albeit without his conscious knowledge, and he couldn't stop replaying the memory.

Aaaannnnd cue the boner.

Goddamn.

Erik would set him on fire if he knew what kind of thoughts he was having about his little sister.

Hey, it's not as if she's a kid, a voice protested in his head. Likely the same part of his brain in charge of his downstairs region. Layton pushed at his growing erection with irritation and an increasing sense of frustration. He wasn't going to jerk off on his buddy's couch. *Just go to sleep.* Tomorrow would come soon enough and he could bail. Right about now he wished he'd just ignored Erik's offer to stay and taken his chances on the road.

Erik was his buddy, a good man and a better firefighter. They shared the same shift and looked out for one another and that meant he couldn't start looking cross-eyed at the guy's sister.

Layton tossed back the blankets and climbed from the couch, needing aspirin for his head. Padding quietly into the kitchen, he began opening cabinets in search of a painkiller when a voice at his back made him turn.

"Okay, I'm willing to overlook the fact that you climbed into my bed without asking, but now you're rummaging through my cabinets? Should I be worried? If I find you going through my underwear drawer next, we're not going to be friends."

Alexis stood there, wrapped in a filmy robe that wasn't much more coverage than the shirt and panties she'd been sporting earlier, and he wondered what he'd done in a past life to deserve such a test. He also noticed she was still favoring her right foot.

"Just looking for aspirin. Someone hit me in the head with a shoe," he responded, trying to keep his eyes from straying. "You really did a number on that ankle. You ought to have it checked out."

"It's nothing. I twisted it a little when I was chasing after you. It'll be fine by morning."

"Are you sure? Sprains can do some damage."

"I'll take that under consideration." Alexis limped in his direction and went to the last cabinet to retrieve some aspirin. She tossed the bottle his way and he caught it with a small smile.

"Thanks," he said.

"Sure." She waited as he shook out two. "So…sorry about the shoe. It was the first thing I could grab and I thought you might be a murderer."

"How many murderers stop to take a snooze before they do their murdering?" he asked, tossing back the aspirin with a swig of water straight from the tap. He wiped his mouth. "I mean, if you really think about it, highly unlikely that I was a murderer."

"Logic and reason don't play when you're jolted out of a dead sleep."

"Okay, I'll give you that," he conceded, wondering if she was going to mention the other thing that happened. What was the protocol on something like this? Should they pretend they hadn't been wrapped in each other's arms, about to do the deed if they hadn't woken up? Sobering thought, even if she was sexy as hell. "So why are you up?"

"Funny thing about getting an adrenaline shot laced with pure survival instinct…hard to sleep after that."

"Sorry," he said. "I should feel guilty, right?"

"A little."

"I do feel bad," he admitted. "I mean… I didn't know you were in the bed. I'm not that kind of guy."

She nodded, accepting his apology, and they both knew he wasn't only talking about the mishap with her ankle.

"Don't worry about it. I've done worse and been just fine. Thanks for caring." A small smile played on those luscious, pouty lips and he had to remind himself that

she was off limits. But he couldn't seem to stop himself from thinking about things that were better kicked
to the curb. Alexis limped to the fridge. "However,
when I can't sleep, I drink warm milk. Want some?"

Yuck. "Not since I was a toddler," he quipped. "But
by all means, help yourself. Don't let me get in the way."

"I won't." Alexis grinned more broadly. Yeah, firecracker was right. This gal was all sass and vinegar
wrapped in a sizzling package of hips and luscious
breasts. Thank God he was leaving in the morning or
he might be sorely tempted to see if she tasted just as
good when he was awake as when he was dreaming.
Alexis poured a mugful and stuck it in the microwave.
"So, how long have you and Erik been friends?"

"Awhile. Same shift. Makes for tight friendships
under the right circumstances. He's a cool dude."

"He is a very cool dude, but then I'm biased."

The microwave dinged and she retrieved her mug
of milk. "You're really going to drink that?" he asked,
grimacing.

"Every drop."

"All right then." He watched her leave and damn
if his eyes didn't go straight to her ass. Yeah…it was
definitely a good thing he was leaving as soon as the
roads were clear. He was only human and he really
didn't want to lose Erik as a friend.

But Alexis Matheson was going to haunt his dreams.

3

ALEXIS WOKE EARLY in spite of the night's events, but mostly because Emma was already up and showered, anxious to hit the road.

"Aren't you a bowl of sunshine?" Alexis said, yawning. "Did you sleep okay? I mean, after everything?"

"Slept fine. But I'm sad to report that you still steal the covers. If I hadn't wrapped myself up like a burrito, you'd have left me with nothing."

Alexis laughed softly. "Bad habits are hard to break. Sorry."

"It's okay, I still love you, but I feel bad for whoever you marry. It's always going to be a battle for the bedding."

"True story." Alexis climbed from the bed, stiff, and still not quite awake. She needed coffee and quick. She swung her legs over the edge of the bed, but as soon as she put pressure on her right foot, she nearly yelped from the shock of pain. *Well, if that isn't a fine way to wake up.* She lifted her ankle and grimaced at the black-and-blue bruising and swelling. *Crap, this doesn't bode well*. Alexis tried to put some pressure on her ankle, but it was a no go. She bit her lip. "Em? We have a problem."

Emma plainly hadn't heard Alexis. "Can you be ready to hit the road in about an hour? I think the roads should be open by then," Emma called out from the bathroom where she was doing her hair.

"Em? Come here a minute," Alexis said, sinking back down on the bed. When Emma appeared with a concerned frown, Alexis said flatly, "Houston, we have a problem."

"What's wrong?" But just as the question left her mouth, her gaze fastened on the nasty bruising on Alexis's ankle and she gasped. "Oh my God! Oh no! That looks terrible, Lex. We need to take you to the doctor. It definitely looks worse."

Alexis had to agree, but she wasn't about to ruin Emma's weekend by spending it in the ER. "It's the weekend, which means an ER visit, and I cannot afford a bill like that right now. I just paid for all my books for the semester. I'm practically living on ramen noodles at this point. I'll just have to wait until my regular doctor's office opens. Besides, what can they do for my foot that I can't?"

"What if it's broken?" Emma fretted.

"It's not broken," Alexis insisted, feeling fairly confident that she was right, but there was a shadow of a doubt that was dogging her. It hurt pretty bad. And the swelling wasn't helping, either. "I probably just need to ice it."

"And elevate it," Emma added with a fatalistic shake

of her head. "There's no way you can sit in the car for the next two hours."

"No. This is not going to ruin our girls' weekend. I've been looking forward to this party for weeks. You know Arnold is going to be crushed if I don't share a cookie with him. I've already promised."

Emma's parents ran a school in Colorado Springs for mentally challenged adults, and Alexis and Emma were planning on surprising Emma's parents at the annual Christmas bash. They were going to serve dinner on Saturday with a full-fledged girls' weekend thrown in the mix.

Alexis enjoyed volunteering at the school. The residents never pretended to be something they weren't— unlike the guys she seemed to attract like bees to pollen.

"Arnold will have to take a rain check," Emma said, then decided, "If you're not going to go to the hospital, then I'm canceling my trip, too. I can't leave you alone like this."

That was exactly what Alexis didn't want Emma to do. "No," Alexis said emphatically. "You are not canceling your trip over this. It's no big deal. It's not as if my foot is going to fall off or something. I just need to baby it a little."

Emma pointed. "Your foot looks like it was beaten with a bat. If it's not broken, I'm willing to guess it's badly sprained."

There was no denying her foot looked terrible. So much for her idea of getting a pedicure. "Please don't cancel on my behalf."

"I can't leave you like this," Emma said, appalled that Alexis would even suggest it.

"Seriously, I'll just putter around the house and watch a movie marathon all day. There's no need for you to cancel your plans because of this, and I would feel ten times worse if you did."

But Emma knew her too well and called her out. "No you won't. You'll try to hang lights and bake and decorate the Christmas tree because you can't stand to sit still. You have the attention span of a gnat and an inability to sit still for any length of time. I'd have to tie you to a chair if I wanted you to stay off that foot."

"That's a little extreme." Alexis pretended to appear offended. "For your information, I recently took up crocheting and that takes a lot of patience."

"You tried it once and then got frustrated and haven't touched it since."

"Okay, fine. Crocheting isn't my thing. But neither is yoga and you're the one who told me to find something to help me relax."

"Yes, and you're still looking because you have a hard time being still. So, forgive me if I don't believe you when you say that you'll take it easy."

Alexis knew Emma was right, but it killed her to think that Emma would cancel over something so dumb. Miserable for ruining her friend's weekend, she rose on unsteady legs with the intent of hobbling her pathetic self to the kitchen for some coffee, but Emma was already slipping her arm beneath her to help. "I'm sorry," Alexis said, feeling like doggie poo. "I didn't mean to ruin our weekend."

"It's okay."

But it wasn't okay. Alexis could hear the sharp disappointment in Emma's voice even as she tried to hide it with a cheerful smile. That was Emma in a nutshell, always thinking of others before herself and it broke Alexis's heart that she was the cause of Emma's disappointment.

Erik and Layton were in the kitchen getting coffee when Emma and Alexis made their way in.

Erik frowned. "Lex? Is that ankle still bothering you?" he asked.

"It hasn't gotten any better," she answered glumly as her butt found a dining room chair. Her mood was rapidly plummeting as quickly as the temperature outside. Another storm was coming. "It actually seems to have gotten worse during the night."

Layton came forward. "Let me take a look."

"It's fine."

But Erik chimed in, saying, "Let Layton take a look, Lex. He's got paramedic training."

Hard to argue with that, seeing as she didn't want to rush to the hospital. "Fine," she grumbled, allowing Layton to gently examine her foot. He slowly manipulated her ankle, carefully gauging her reaction. She winced a few times and then yelped when he pressed her foot. Layton nodded and released her foot with care. "Well, I don't think it's broken, but you've probably got one helluva sprain. If you go to the ER they'll order an X-ray, which won't show soft-tissue damage, but it'll definitively show whether or not you have a fracture."

"But you don't think it's broken, right?" Alexis said.

"I don't, but that doesn't mean you couldn't have a hairline fracture. Best to check it out."

"See?" Emma said, lightly tapping Alexis's head for being difficult. "I'll drive you to the hospital."

"No, I'm not going to the hospital," she said stubbornly. "And you're not missing out on your parents' bash. Erik, please tell Emma that I'm a big girl and I can handle myself, even slightly injured."

"Lex, it's fine, really. I don't really want to drive alone anyway, so we'll just do that movie marathon you mentioned. It'll be fun."

"Erik can go with you," Alexis volunteered, shocking Emma. She didn't know why she'd offered her brother's services, but it seemed to make sense. Erik was a total gentleman.

"Oh! That's not necessary. I'm sure he has plans," Emma said, darting a look at Erik. "It's fine, really. I don't mind canceling. Lex really shouldn't be alone with her foot the way it is."

Alexis sent an imploring look Erik's way, *C'mon, bro, don't let me down!*

But it was Layton who spoke up first. "I can't believe I'm going to say this, but… I could stay behind and help you out so your friend doesn't feel like you're being left behind all alone. It's kind of my fault you're all banged up anyway."

All eyes turned to Layton. Did Layton just volunteer to babysit her?

Erik said, "That's okay, man. You don't have to do that. It's not your fault. It was a misunderstanding all the way around."

"I know, but hell, I've got nothing to do today that

didn't include drinking a few beers and being a slug. Besides, I've got the training. If her ankle gets worse, I'll bundle her up and force her to go to the ER."

"He has a point," Erik slowly agreed, nodding. Then he looked to Emma. "How do you feel about that?"

Alexis hesitated then looked to Erik and Emma, saying, "Well, if Erik agreed to go with Emma… I guess that would solve both problems. Are you okay with that, Em?" As soon as the words left her mouth, Emma started shaking her head, but Alexis wasn't going to budge on this one. "Em, it's dangerous on the roads. You know it's stupid to drive alone and I refuse to let you cancel your plans. Erik will be the perfect gentleman, I can promise. He's one of the good guys."

Emma's cheeks flared as her gaze darted. "I know Erik is a good guy. I just don't want him to have to do something he doesn't want to do."

Erik chimed in. "I don't mind," he said. "And I agree with Lex. You shouldn't drive alone in these conditions."

"The storm doesn't seem to be letting up as I'd hoped," Emma said, biting her lip with indecision. "Are you sure you don't mind the drive?"

"Not at all. We can catch up. Tell me what's new in your life since you were just my bratty little sister's friend."

"Bratty?" Alexis repeated with indignation. "Like you were the epitome of well behaved. Just because Mom and Dad were blind to your antics doesn't mean everyone was. For your information, I told them that it was you who broke Mom's ceramic elephant from Africa during that party you held your senior year."

"You little snitch. You promised you wouldn't tell. I paid good hush money for that," Erik said, grinning. "I should've threatened some kind of punishment for reneging on the deal."

"Good times," Alexis said, laughing. "Okay, so is it settled? Erik will go with Emma, and Layton will stay with me?"

They all shared looks and then nodded, agreeing. Emma heaved a breath and then said, "All right, if that's the case, we need to get moving. If that storm is determined to dump another load of snow, I want to put some miles on the road before it happens."

"I can be ready to roll in fifteen minutes. That work for you?"

Emma nodded and they both split off to finish getting ready.

"And just like that, it was you and me," Layton said.

"Yeah…you know you don't actually need to stay," she said in a conspiratorial whisper. "I appreciate what you did. Emma wouldn't have agreed without Erik and you volunteering. As soon as they take off, wait about a half hour and then you can take off, too."

He shook his head, grinning. "Sorry, no can do. My offer was legit. What kind of guy would I be if I left you to fend for yourself when you're plainly injured?"

That surprised her. He really wanted to stay? To be truthful, she'd thought he was just giving her backup. "Seriously?"

"Yeah, I mean, I know it's not actually my fault, but I do feel a bit responsible for your laid-up foot. The least I can do to assuage my guilt is to help you out."

Alexis didn't know what to say to that. She paused

for the tiniest of moments only because a hot guy was her personal weakness, and the last person she needed to mess around with was her brother's best friend, but what were the odds that anything would happen between them over a weekend? She could be around a hot guy and keep her hands to herself. She smiled with determination—mostly to prove something to herself—and said, "Okay, but don't say I didn't warn you. I wasn't lying when I said I had a movie marathon in mind."

"I like movies."

"Chick flicks."

"Movies with hot chicks? Sounds good to me."

She laughed at his devilish charm. Yeah, he was just the sort of guy who'd turn her head. But not this time. Nope.

Layton Davis...it ain't gonna happen.

TRUE TO HIS WORD, Erik was ready to go within twenty minutes. With Emma in her SUV waiting, Erik paused to give the obligatory big-brother speech, which Layton didn't fault him for, but he was tempted to remind Erik that Alexis wasn't a kid.

"I know you're a good guy or else I wouldn't even think of leaving Alexis with you, but I feel I have to warn you about my sister. She's...spirited."

Layton's brow rose. "Spirited? Erik...*horses* are spirited. Be more specific."

"Hell, this is the most awkward conversation ever. Look, she has a thing for falling for the wrong guy and I don't want to see her hurt. She's been through enough. Her last boyfriend... Let's just say I wasn't a fan. So, yeah, what I'm trying to say is…don't mess with her and for God's sake, don't let her mess with you. Keep things friendly, but not too friendly."

"C'mon, man, like you would have to ask. I'm not here to hook up with your sister. I'm just helping out."

The look of relief pinged Layton's conscience. The fact was, Alexis was hot. She was a grade-A hot piece of ass if he were being honest, but he meant what he'd said. He wasn't here to mess around with the woman.

Erik clapped him on the shoulder and climbed into the car. "Help yourself to whatever's in the fridge. I'll call you when we get there."

"Drive safe," Layton said, waving.

The snow started to drift lazily from the sky, dissolving into tiny wet spots on his face almost instantly. He glanced at the sky. Hopefully, they made good time before the storm really started up again. Layton turned on his heel and returned to the house, where Alexis was already up and hopping around the kitchen.

"What are you doing?"

"Nothing. What are you doing?"

"Preventing you from overdoing it. What happened to the movie marathon?"

"There's plenty of time for that. I want to make some kettle corn. Want some?"

Kettle corn. How did she know it was his weakness? "You know how to make it?"

"I sure hope so, otherwise I'm about to make a huge mess for nothing."

He chuckled. "Okay, wiseass, as much as I would love to scarf down some kettle corn, you are getting off that foot. I told you I didn't think it was broken, but it's certainly sprained and you need to elevate it with some ice."

Alexis scowled, but he didn't give her a chance to argue and simply scooped her into his arms, shocking her into stunned silence as he carried her to the living room. He deposited her on the sofa and then put a pillow under her foot. "You sit here while I get the ice."

"Is now the appropriate time to admit that Emma was right and that I don't sit still well?"

"I already had that figured out."

"Story of my life. I've never been able to just sit around. Once I had the chicken pox and I drove my mother crazy because I couldn't stop itching and squirming, which then made it worse. My mom says it was the longest two weeks of her life."

Alexis's story was telling. He held no illusions that Alexis would be an easy patient, but there was something about her that drew him, in spite of all the reasons he ought to keep his distance. Maybe it was the memory of those dream kisses or maybe it was the memory of that near-perfect ass. Ha! Neither memory was safe enough to entertain for longer than a heartbeat.

He returned with an icepack wrapped in a towel and gently draped it on Alexis's ankle. "That ought to help, but you really have to keep off your foot if you want it to heal."

"Yeah, yeah," she grumbled. "Are you sure you want to hang around? There's nothing exciting about watching paint dry."

"Depends on the company."

Alexis met his gaze and cocked her head to the side

with a sweet, beguiling grin that he didn't trust in the least but found extremely compelling. "Is that so? And are you saying that you would enjoy my company? The woman who nearly turned you from a rooster to a hen with one kick?"

"In spite of that…yeah."

Were they flirting? It felt like flirting. And he liked it.

Hell, he'd always been a sucker for the girl who was just out of reach; she didn't need to make it ten times more difficult by being sexy, too.

Erik's advice rang in his head like a gong and he pulled back even though there was something captivating about Alexis—and he wasn't just talking about the sweet rack she was sporting.

"You're going to get me into trouble," he said with a chuckle as he rose from his haunches. "You know your brother has it in his head that you're this fragile thing who might break if handled too roughly." He waited a heartbeat, then asked with a sly grin, "What do you think about that?"

She met his grin with a saucy one of her own. "I think I'm a big girl and I don't need my brother to run interference for me."

"That may be true, but I'm not the kind of guy who would go behind a buddy's back to get at his sister. You know what I mean?"

"That's admirable," she admitted with grudging respect.

"And why does it feel the opposite when you say it like that?"

She laughed and the sound tickled his bones like

fingertips dancing down his vertebrae. "I told you, you don't have to stay. I'll be fine."

"I gave your brother my word. I'm not going anywhere."

There was the slightest, most minute, almost indiscernible hitch in her breath, and that sexy little sound almost caused an immediate erection to tent his jeans. Ah hell, this was going to be the hardest test of his life. For crying out loud, they'd only just met, but there was electricity bouncing between them that was hard to ignore, and if she didn't stop looking at him as if he were the choicest cut of beef, he was going to have a helluva time keeping to his word.

"Tell me about this guy who did you wrong," he said, moving to sit beside her on the sofa. Act like a friend. Not a hungry wolf ready to pounce. "According to Erik, he was a douche."

"He said that?"

"Well, not in so many words, but I got the impression he hadn't thought much of him."

She shrugged as if it was no big deal, but beneath that negligent shrug was the faint show of heartache that surprised him. Alexis gave off the vibe that if anyone was doing the heartbreaking, it was her and not the other way around.

"What can I say? I'm a terrible judge of character," she said.

"I don't believe that."

"No? Well, I can't deny that I've been drawn to the worst sort of guy. My track record isn't the best."

"We all have unfortunate hookups in our past," he said. "It's called live and learn."

Alexis laughed and adjusted the ice pack. "Yeah, well, until I get through with my master's degree there will only be one kind of learning going on."

"Sounds like a solid plan."

And it was. So why did he want to make her break it?

4

CIRCUMSTANCE WAS A funny thing. Alexis stared at her ankle, amazed at how much could change in the blink of an eye. Last night she was lobbing objects at Layton's head and today, she was noticing how nicely his cropped, dark hair set off the masculine cut of his jaw. Maybe she wouldn't mind if Layton played nursemaid after all. Even if she had the very best intentions to keep her hands to herself, she could certainly enjoy the view.

And the view was quite spectacular. Muscled chest and arms, solid abs narrowing to a trim waist and hips... Yes, indeed, Layton had the goods.

"Okay, so tell me the real reason you volunteered to stay behind," Alexis said, putting Layton on the spot, trying to make things interesting.

"What makes you think I wasn't being completely altruistic in my offer?"

"Were you?"

Layton paused, then that little glint in his wondrously dark eyes gave him away. "Okay, full disclosure…you're a beautiful woman and I happen to have a weakness for women like you, but even with that said… I promised your brother that I wouldn't do or say anything inappropriate."

"Such a gentleman," she murmured as her heart rate did a little jump at his admission. Was it terrible that she was already imagining him naked beneath her? Good grief, her hormones were out of control.

"I wouldn't go that far," he said ruefully. "I'd be a liar if I didn't admit that keeping my thoughts on the straight and narrow has already proven to be a challenge."

She smiled, enjoying that she wasn't the only one thinking about inappropriate things. "Seems we have more than my brother in common," she returned.

"Careful, those kinds of comments are dangerous."

"To whom? Because I'm an adult and don't need a chaperone."

He laughed. "I promised your brother."

"That was your mistake."

"Hot damn, Erik warned me about you and it seems he was right on the money."

"Did he? And what exactly did he warn you about?"

"Just that you have a taste for trouble and that I ought to steer clear."

She pouted. "That's not flattering at all. Makes me sound like a kid."

"You are definitely no kid," he said, his gaze feasting on her ample breasts. If there was one asset she knew she owned, it was her impressive cup size. He cleared his throat as if he realized that he was staring and actually made a concentrated effort to look elsewhere. "But I've gotta hold on to a shred of integrity, you know?"

"So noble."

He smirked. "Well, I respect the hell out of your brother. He's a good man. I'm not about to start looking at his sister like a piece of meat."

"Is that one of the lesser-known 'Bro Code' rules?" she teased.

"Call it what you want, it's just how I operate."

"You're playing into that firefighter-hero stereotype pretty hard," she said with a mischievous smile, enjoying their banter. "I wonder if there's a bad boy lurking underneath that polished exterior."

He chuckled, the sound tickling her senses. "You have no idea."

Was she completely wicked that she suddenly had a desperate hunger to find out just how bad Layton could be? Probably. Particularly when she'd made a pact with herself to keep on the straight and narrow until she had her master's. It was a good plan at the time. Now? Seemed stupid as hell.

"What would you say if I told you I was attracted to you?"

He held his easy smile, but something in his gaze changed and her body tingled with awareness. "Then I'd say that you'd better keep that on lockdown because things could get awkward."

She could call his bluff. Alexis knew when a guy was into her. Layton was throwing off signals that a person would have to be blind not to see, but she felt a bit like a predator chasing after a poor doomed gazelle. He was plainly telling her it wasn't going to happen and she respected that—to a point—but his gaze was also throwing sparks that were bound to catch fire at some point.

Alexis sighed dramatically, leaning casually against the sofa, idly gazing at her injured foot. "Well, the truth of the matter is the fact that I want to give you a tongue bath must mean that somewhere, deep down, you're defective."

He startled with a laugh. "I think you just insulted me, but for the life of me all I can think of is that tongue bath."

"See? It's hopeless. Let's be honest, we're both adults and we're both attracted to one another. We also both know that we shouldn't act upon the dirty thoughts in our heads. So…it's probably best that you go home before something terribly unfortunate happens between us."

"Unfortunate?"

"Yeah, like all our clothes flying off and landing on the floor."

He swallowed and she privately delighted in the way the thought made him stutter a little. "Are you always this blunt?"

"Pretty much. My mom says I've always suffered from a lack of tact, but my dad says I don't seem to suffer from it at all."

Layton laughed with a slight twinkle in his eye that she found highly alluring. "Okay, well, not leaving. I made a promise to Erik that I'd stick around and make sure you stayed off that foot, so you're just going to have to deal with my company."

Alexis held his gaze for a moment then shrugged.

"Okay, but I can't be held responsible for what may happen between us."

"Nothing is going to happen," he said with amused laughter. "You don't quit, do you? You're like a dog with a bone."

Alexis shrugged. "We'll see."

"How about this? You pick the movie and I'll scramble up some eggs and bacon for breakfast."

She perked up. The only thing capable of jarring her one-track mind was the introduction of her second favorite distraction: food. "You can cook?"

"A necessary skill when you live with a bunch of other guys several days out of the week. Yes, I can cook. Any requests?"

Oh, how could she not take him up on that offer? She hated to cook but she loved to eat. "A Denver omelet would be fab," she admitted. "I think we have everything you need in the fridge."

"Denver omelet coming up," Layton said, going to the kitchen. "And while I'm making breakfast you can throw out movie ideas."

On the surface, that sounded well and good, but Alexis didn't want to sit around the house all day. She spent so much of her time studying that she needed a physical outlet. Her gaze drifted to the window where soft snowflakes fell lazily from the sky. The storm hadn't hit yet. There was probably just enough time to get the lights up before the snow really started coming down.

Maybe she could convince Layton to help her string the lights? But how to do it was the question.

She wasn't above using her charm to get what she

wanted and she had a feeling Layton wouldn't mind fresh air…once he realized that spending too much time cuddled up on the sofa wasn't a good idea, particularly if he was determined to keep things Disney-rated.

Before too long, Layton returned with two plates of omelets and toast, and Alexis's opinion of her brother's friend went up a notch.

"Did you pick out a movie?"

"No, I did something better," she said around a bite of omelet. "Oh, that's good. You're a handy guy to have around. Cute, built like a Roman god and can cook? Okay, just level with me, what's your hidden defect?"

"I have a weakness for pretty, sass-mouthed women," he admitted wryly as he shoveled in his food.

"How much of a weakness?" she asked, curious.

Layton leveled a wry look her way. "Enough of one. Eat your breakfast."

"So bossy."

"Has anyone ever successfully told you what to do?"

She affected a serious expression. "My dad." But she couldn't keep a straight face for long, laughing as she said, "But you're not my dad so don't even try to boss me around."

"Duly noted." He gestured to her plate. "Good?"

"Fan-freaking-tastic," Alexis openly admitted with glee. "You're quite a catch. So tell me, Layton, do you chase the ladies or do the ladies chase you?"

Layton gave her a sideways grin that showcased a nice row of white, even teeth. The man could audition for a toothpaste commercial without an ounce of reservation. "I've chased my share, but I've been chased, too."

"It's all about the chase though, isn't it? Once you've gotten what you want...where's the mystery? Where's the thrill?" She couldn't help a twist of hidden bitterness to shape her words. Maybe she was still smarting from her last boyfriend. He'd been all about the chase, too.

But Layton frowned, shaking his head. "Some guys are like that. I'm not."

Alexis barked a laugh, not believing him for a second. "You don't have to put on an act for me. I know guys are all about getting laid."

"When I'm with a girl, I only have eyes for her," he said with such seriousness that she paused for a moment, thrown off track. How could a man who looked like Layton be a one-woman kind of guy? She didn't buy it. "Seriously?"

He shrugged as if he didn't care if she believed him or not. "The chase is fun, don't get me wrong, but the real good stuff? That happens after you get to know each other. Never underestimate the value of being able to be yourself with your partner."

"Whoa there, Dr. Phil," Alexis joked, a little uncomfortable with how quickly things had gotten serious. "I was just kidding."

But she wasn't entirely. Riker had screwed up her internal sensor so badly she wasn't sure it worked any longer and she didn't trust her own judgment. Sure, Layton seemed like a good guy, but didn't they all in the beginning? It was better to keep things superficial than risk getting hurt later. She'd happily step over the line and break her own rule for the opportunity for some hot blow-your-mind sex, but that's where it stopped.

"For what it's worth, you don't have to try to convince me that you're not a player. I don't really care one way or the other."

"Why is it so hard to believe that I'm a good guy?"

"Because I've known too many guys like you to know better," she quipped.

But Layton set her straight with a quiet "Something tells me you've never met a guy like me."

He said it with such confidence that for a split second Alexis stopped to wonder if he was telling the truth. But wasn't that the problem? She always thought they were being truthful until that terrible moment when she discovered otherwise. She was done with being played. "You can drop the act, buddy. I'm not interested in the game. I mean, I'm down for a little fun, but I don't need the white lies to smooth the way."

Layton frowned, shaking his head with faint irritation. "Boy, Erik wasn't wrong. You must've been screwed over big-time to be so jaded at such a young age. So, for the sake of every other man that happens to cross your path, why don't you tell me what happened with this other dude so I can assure you that not every guy is like that."

He wanted to listen? Alexis covered her surprise with an airy laugh. His comment hit too close to home for comfort. Riker's betrayal still stung. But she didn't feel like opening up her chest and revealing her broken heart to a complete stranger. Sex was one thing—being vulnerable was another.

"Okay, Mr. Wonderful…why don't you have a girl-friend?"

Layton leaned forward to put his plate on the coffee table. "Guess I'm taking a break from it all."

"What do you mean?"

"The dating thing. I'm over it."

She handed him her plate and he set it on top of his. "Explain."

Layton shook his head with a small smile and then went to gently lift the ice pack from her foot. "I'm tired of the game. First dates, the obligatory small talk, the uncertainty of the outcome…it's all one colossal drag on my time. I'd rather spend it hiking or riding my bike than sitting across the table from someone I just met to try to make some kind of connection. I don't know…just not into it right now."

Alexis laughed. "Okay, so it seems I'm not the only one who's been burned in the past."

"Touché."

"What was her name?"

"What was his?"

"Riker."

Layton did a double take. "Riker?" he repeated with a fair amount of incredulity. "Well, there's your prob-lem right there. Anyone name Riker is bound to be trouble."

She couldn't argue that point. "He was hot."

"So was she."

Alexis laughed, strangely enjoying the way they both flirted around the edges of something person-ally painful without poking too hard for the other's comfort. If she were being truthful, she was terribly curious about the woman who'd been stupid enough to break this man's heart.

If she were smart, she'd keep everything surface level.

But then if she were smart, she wouldn't be in this position anyway, so why start now?

5

THAT SASS WAS ADDICTIVE.

Alexis was a ball of contradictions. Hot and spirited and yet, beneath all that burning sex appeal was a girl who'd obviously been hurt enough to withdraw from anything or anyone who might be able to hurt her again.

He could understand Erik wanting to punch the last boyfriend's lights out, because he was feeling a little punchy himself and he had no reason to.

But turnabout was fair play so he let loose with a little intel. "All right…you shared, so I'll give you something in return. Her name was Julianne. Jules for short."

Alexis snapped her fingers with a definitive shake of her head. "Yep. Gotta steer clear of anyone named Jules—immediate problem."

"Is that so?"

"Absolutely. You should also avoid anyone named Tiffany or Brittany and if they spell their names with an *i* run like hell."

"Good advice." He nodded, adding for her benefit, "Conversely, any guy named after a *Star Trek Next Gen* character you should avoid like the plague. Born players. They're all concerned with going 'where no man has gone before.'"

Alexis broke into peals of laughter, prompting a grin of his own. She had a way about her that was un-abashed and free, definitely different from most girls he met, and it was getting harder to remember why he was supposed to keep his distance.

"Any other advice you might want to impart from the other side of the curtain?" she asked playfully.

He made a show of thinking, but all he was really thinking was that he wanted to kiss her. Strands of dark hair escaped her low ponytail to curl around her jaw, but she made no move to fix it and he was glad. There was something about her devil-may-care atti-tude about her hair that he found refreshing. Jules had always been picture-perfect, or at least worked hard to appear so and it got old. *Don't touch my hair* or *don't smudge my lipstick* were familiar admonishments be-fore the end had come crashing down around them. "How's your ankle feeling?" he asked, redirecting his own thoughts to safer ground.

Alexis's gaze dropped to her ankle and she nodded. "Better. The ice helped."

"You should still stay off it," he said, trying to stay focused. "Now…are we going to watch movies or what?"

"Is there a third option?"

"Such as?"

"Such as…hanging lights."

"Come again?"

"Here's the deal, I can't sit here for hours on end and just zone out. I need to be doing something, and since I'm stuck home when I thought I'd be elsewhere, and since you've already shared that you don't think it's a good idea if we knock boots, that leads me to suggest that you help me hang lights…seeing as I'm laid up and all." She paused for effect then added, "Or, I suppose we *could* stay indoors, cuddled up on the sofa… just you and me and no one else in the house…with total privacy to do *whatever* we wanted and *no one* would ever know…"

"You don't play fair," he groaned, his groin immediately jumping into the conversation, happy to join the fun, which was a terrible, bad thing in the way of trying to keep his hands where they belonged—off Alexis!

"I never said I played fair," she said with a beguiling smile. "I play to win."

Damn straight, she did. He had to respect that. His choices were: ignore his better judgment and allow Alexis to hop around outside hanging lights or keep her indoors and try to be a good guy and keep his hands to himself. Yeah, not much of a choice. He wasn't a damn saint. He gave in with a sigh. "All right, you win this round. I suppose being outside doing something is better than staring temptation straight in the face with you cuddled up beside me. But on one condition…"

"Which is?" she asked warily.

"You sit your ass in a chair and let me do the work. The last thing I need is your brother asking why I let you hop around on an injured foot and you end up hurting yourself worse."

She made a face. "You make me sound like an invalid. I'm fine. However, I concede to your demands. I will direct the labor and you will do the heavy lifting."

He chuckled and grabbed the dishes. "So when is this decorating frenzy scheduled to begin?"

"Well, in the interest of not being outside when that storm hits, I'd say about five minutes after you put away the dishes and we get dressed. Sound good?"

Layton agreed, and she was actually ready to go a minute earlier than he was. He gave her a once-over ostensibly to gauge whether or not she was dressed warmly enough, but actually, his gaze was far from simply friendly. Hot damn. That girl could melt snow. White fuzzy boots, white fur-lined jacket and white snow pants, she looked like a snow bunny from an upscale ski resort who didn't plan to actually do any skiing but would look plenty cute just sitting in the lodge sipping hot chocolate. "Trying to blend in with the snow?" he teased, needing desperately to treat her like a little sister so he stopped seeing her as a full-fledged woman with hips and curves. "I'm not sure you have enough white."

She fake scowled. "Pardon me if I don't take fashion tips from a man who thinks pajama pants are acceptable for going out in public."

"Correction—*lounge* pants. Not pajamas," he said, adding with a wink because he couldn't help himself. "As you've already discovered, I sleep in the nude. No need for pajamas."

Her cheeks flared adorably and he had to admit it

did nice things to his ego. *Knock it off, Romeo. Erik's little sister, remember?* Layton reined in his giddy libido with effort. "Okay, show me where the lights are and let's get this started." If Alexis sensed the fact that he was struggling with the need to be the good guy, she didn't let on and he was thankful. He was quickly becoming a powder keg and she was the match. Just how would Erik react if he found out that the guy he'd left his injured little sister with had ended up boning her like some jerk-off who couldn't keep his dick in his pants for one damn day. Yeah, Layton knew exactly how he'd react—badly.

And with good reason.

Layton hefted the box of lights from the garage and followed Alexis's instructions, bringing three big boxes from their storage spot to the front porch.

"I'll test the strands, you hang," she said cheerfully, her breath pluming in front of her as her eyes sparkled. "I'm so glad I'm getting a chance to hang these a bit earlier than expected. Typically, I like the lights to go up right after Thanksgiving, but with midterms and a brutal professor who seems to hate me, I've been knee-deep in school stuff."

"So master's degree...that's pretty impressive."

She grinned broadly. "My dad calls me the perpetual student. He swears my decision to get my master's was to get out of finding a real job."

"Was it?"

Alexis gasped with mock outrage. "Of course not. I just want to land at the top of the food chain, and the only way to do that is with a master's degree."

"You want to be the boss?"

She looked wistful and aggressive at the same time as she nodded. "Hell yes. I don't know if you could tell, but I'm not the type of person who takes orders very well. I'm much better at giving than following them."

Why did he just think of her giving orders in bed? And why the hell did he find that idea hot as hell? *Get your head in the game and focus, Layton! Thoughts like that are gonna land your ass in a pan of boiling water.*

"The world takes all sorts," he said with a forced grin, watching as she tested the first strand. Satisfied when all the lights twinkled and blinked, she handed the strand off to him and moved onto the next. He took the light hooks and began lining them along the porch rafters so he could hook the strand into each one. "Okay, so don't take this the wrong way but you don't seem the Suzy Homemaker type. What's with the driving need to decorate for Christmas?"

"Christmas is my favorite holiday and always has been," she answered with a small shrug. "There's just something about the holiday that recharges my battery and restores my faith in humanity."

"Christmas does that for you?" he asked incredulously. "That's funny, all I see are a bunch of people trying to screw each other over for material stuff."

"Sure, that happens, but what about the stories of people who go out of their way to help a stranger?"

"Yeah, I suppose that's nice."

"You suppose?"

"No, that didn't come out right…it is nice. I guess I just don't see enough of that. Christmas always seemed the greediest time of year. Really turned me off the holiday."

"That's a tragedy."

He shrugged. "Nah, it's just life. I like St. Patrick's Day, if it means anything."

"And why is that?" she asked.

"Because it's a day sanctioned for drinking beer." She rolled her eyes and he grinned, adding, "Can't imagine a better holiday than that." Layton held the strand, inspecting it for loose wires of any sort as a force of habit. "Actually, I'd be lying if I said that I don't enjoy Christmas a little bit. I like the lights and the displays but I've seen too many house fires caused by Christmas trees that it's hard to forget what's left behind."

Alexis sobered, pausing in her strand detail. "That must suck."

"It does. I don't want to be a Debbie Downer, but Christmastime…can be kind of scary for public service. Do you realize that suicides and domestic violence go up during the holidays?"

"You're a bowl of sunshine," she said, handing him the strand. "You should really think of going into inspirational speaking."

"Sorry. Occupational hazard, I guess."

"You're forgiven, but I don't care what you say, nothing can dim my holiday spirit. I love the holiday and I'm determined to enjoy every last moment."

Layton had to respect her determination to get her Christmas on, no matter the obstacles.

"One question though."

"Yeah?"

"Why are you decorating your brother's place? Is he as nutty about the holidays as you are?"

"Gracious no. Erik is about as observant as a lawn gnome. He's not much into the whole decorating thing, which is why he lets me do what I want. Someday I'll have my own place and I'll be able to stop commandeering my brother's place."

"Heaven help the man you settle down with. I can only imagine what your house is going to look like."

"It's going to be fabulous and whoever I end up with will be the luckiest guy in the world because I make the world's most insanely delicious gingerbread-men cookies and I give a pretty hot blow job."

Layton stumbled back, missing the step and going down hard on his ass in the snow.

"Are you all right?" she asked, barely holding back her laughter.

"I'm fine," he grumbled, climbing to his feet and wiping the loose snow from his pants. "You shouldn't say things like that to a man you barely know."

Alexis smiled with the innocence of an angel, but that impish twist at the corners of her lips ruined it in the most tantalizing way.

"Just stating facts." She held out the next strand as if she hadn't just rung his bell hard. "Better hurry, that storm is moving quick."

"Are you the devil?" he muttered, mostly to himself, but she heard him loud and clear.

"Not the devil but quite possibly a fallen angel."

A fallen angel with an agenda.

And he was running out of willpower to stay the course.

Heaven help him, what had he gotten himself into?

6

ALEXIS KNEW THE minute the words came out of her mouth that she shouldn't have said them. What was wrong with her? It was as if she were bound and determined to make the worst mistake of her life in record time.

"I'm sorry," she said, quickly making amends. "I shouldn't have said that. It was totally inappropriate. I don't know what's wrong with me. My brain is certainly not acting responsibly—not that that's a big surprise given my track record, but I really am trying to change bad habits."

His chuckle seemed forced, but what could she expect after she'd just let her potty mouth get the best of her. "Hey, it's okay," he reassured her. "Don't beat yourself up over it. We've all made mistakes that we're not proud of. Besides, there's nothing wrong with being proud of a skill."

She couldn't help herself. "When you say things like that it makes me not sorry at all."

A beat of charged silence flowed between them,

filling the crisp air with heat. Layton shook his head. "We're a pair to draw to, aren't we?"

"As in, we both have the same problem recognizing what boundaries to pay attention to?"

"Exactly," he agreed ruefully. "I know it's wrong to look at my buddy's little sister the way I'm looking at you now, but it's getting harder and harder to remember why I was supposed to keep my distance."

A delighted flush tickled her cheeks. "And if I wasn't your buddy's little sister?" she prompted.

He didn't hesitate. "Then we sure as hell wouldn't be hanging lights right now."

What he didn't say was plainly in his gaze. Her breath caught. "Maybe we could pretend that I'm not your buddy's little sister. Just for today."

"I'm not sure that would work. Eventually Erik would find out and I really don't want to lose a friend because, you know, I couldn't keep my hands to myself."

It was solid reasoning, and that he was holding back to protect the feelings of a friend meant something, but it really didn't change the fact that she wanted him and she wasn't sure she wanted to deny herself. "I understand and I think it's awesome that you're the kind of guy who cares, but there's something about you that I can't quite get out of my head and maybe it's because I'm in a reckless frame of mind or maybe it's because you're the hottest guy I've seen in a along time, but right about now, I'd much rather spend my weekend making all sorts of mistakes with you than anything else. So what are we going to do about that?"

"You're making it real hard to be good."

"I guess what I'm saying is I'm not interested in you being good this weekend."

"Yeah, but you're not the only one who's been hammered by bad decisions. I'm trying to change, too."

Was it wrong that she couldn't care less about his past or how he was trying to make amends? Okay, so the fact was, her heart was a little broken. Maybe she didn't like to admit it out loud, but she could feel the jagged pieces scraping and poking and sometimes it was just hard to ignore. "Have you ever just wanted to do the exact thing you know is wrong for so many reasons and yet it felt so right?"

"Story of my damn life."

"At least we have that in common. Erik has always been the responsible one, the one who could be counted on, whereas I was the one people always thought of as the flake. I don't want to be that person anymore, but habits are hard to change."

"But not impossible," he told her. "If you want to be a different person, you have to take steps to be that different person. And that means not doing the things that you want to do the most. At least, that's the advice I've been given."

"So why do you want to change so bad?"

"There just comes a time when you realize that you can't keep doing what you've been doing and hope to have a good life at the end of your days. I mean, I don't want to get all sappy, but I want a family at some point. And that's not going to happen if I don't stop chasing after the wrong tail."

"You have a point," she said, trying not to let his admission hit a soft spot, but she wasn't accustomed to hearing men talk about the idea of settling down. "And I don't think that's sappy at all. I think that's really sweet—and shocking—coming from a guy like you."

"Shocking? How so?"

Alexis shrugged. "I don't know, I guess I'm playing into the stereotype, but guys who look like you and are built like you are usually more interested in sowing their oats rather than putting down roots."

He laughed. "Well, a year ago I was definitely the stereotype. For lack of a better word I was a little... *free* with my affections. But I realized the hard way that people were getting hurt. And that's not the person I want to be."

He had no way of knowing, but his statement had just tingled her ovaries as effectively as if he'd clanged a bell. "If I were more of a cynic, I'd say that was the most effective line I've ever heard."

"Not a line, it's the truth. There's only so many times you can do the walk of shame without it affecting you."

"Men do the walk of shame? I thought it was always the woman."

He chuckled. "I don't know, I've done some shameful things."

She laughed. "Am I a bad person that I want to hear details?"

"Not a bad person, but you're not going to get them, either. Those stories are going to go to my grave."

"Okay, now I'm intrigued. I have to make it my goal to crack open that safe."

Layton scooped up the empty boxes and carried them up the porch where Alexis was sitting in a chair.

"And on that note…what else are we going to do out here? I'm about to freeze my balls off."

"No fair. You can't mention body parts if I can't mention skills. But you're off the hook, the lights were all I wanted to do today."

"Good." He carried the boxes into the house, but just as Alexis started to hobble after him he returned and scooped her up as if she weighed nothing.

She gasped, her cheeks warming. "I'm not crippled. I can walk."

"Maybe I just want to feel you or maybe I'm just being a gentleman. Either way, I come out on the winning side when I have a fine woman in my arms."

Couldn't argue that logic. The man had a way with words, and that smile was quickly becoming her weakness. She laughed and enjoyed the feeling of Layton holding her as if she was precious cargo. He returned her to the sofa and elevated her foot. "You know, if this firefighter gig doesn't work out, I think you could have a real future in home health care."

Layton smirked. "I'll keep that in mind. But only if all of my patients look as cute as you."

"Can't make any promises there. I am pretty cute."

"And modest. Dangerous combination."

Layton went to pull away and she snagged his shirt by the lapels and dragged him straight to her lips. "Since we've already agreed we both suck at making good decisions, we might as well just go with it. I'm tired of fighting what I desperately want to do."

And then she sealed her lips to his in a searing kiss so hot that any good sense between the two of them went up in smoke.

Danger! Abort!

Red sirens and flashing neon lights blazed in his conscience, but if there was an angel and devil sitting on either shoulder, the angel had just been duct-taped and hog-tied, because he sure as hell wasn't in charge.

Alexis's skin was like soft silk beneath his fingertips as his tongue danced with hers, the urge to taste every inch of her body burning through his brain like a fever. This was the sweetest, most tantalizing lunacy, but he couldn't stop. Heaven help him, he couldn't stop if he tried.

Her hands, as eager as his own, pushed at his shirt and within seconds he'd ripped off the offending piece of clothing, his skin burning at her insistent touch. He slowed only long enough to help her remove her top and he nearly swallowed his tongue when she revealed the most achingly perfect breasts God had ever created. Sweetly upturned pink nipples pearled and pouted, demanding a hot mouth to suck and tease them and he wasn't about to disappoint.

Wasting no time, he sucked a tightly budded nipple into his mouth and teased the tip with his tongue. Alexis groaned and her belly trembled as his hands kneaded the soft, pliant flesh of her glorious breasts and he knew there was no going back. They were in too deep now. And he wasn't going to think about Erik—hell no, talk about a buzzkill—all he wanted to think about was how to make Alexis squirm in his arms. He wanted to hear her breathy moans in his ear, taste her sweet juices as she came and feel her shudder beneath him.

How did they get here? One minute they were hang-

ing lights—totally platonic, right?—and now, he was
ready to flip the switch and go down on her. "Alexis,
tell me if you want me to stop," he said, hating the
words but needing to say them anyway. They were
playing with fire, but he'd pull back if she said to.

"Don't you dare stop," she growled, pushing at his
head as she shimmied out of her pants, wincing briefly
as she cleared her injured ankle. Following her lead,
he grinned and helped her out of her panties, grabbing
the tiny scrap of lace and inhaling the unique scent.

"Mmm, perfect," he said, unabashedly enjoying
Alexis's unique scent. "God, you smell incredible."

Alexis blushed but seemed to revel in his enjoyment. He grinned and tossed the panties, ready to dive
into the real thing. Everything about Alexis excited
him. At this point he figured he deserved a medal
for holding out as long as he had. He positioned himself between her legs, careful not to jostle her injured
ankle, and then feasted on the honeyed sweetness between her legs. He teased the tiny button nestled between her damp folds, licked and laved the bare flesh,
tickling the tiny strip of pubic hair seaming her cleft.

A breathy shudder escaped her lips as she tensed,
her body shaking almost immediately. Manly pride
surged through him as he sucked and licked her pleasure spot until she stiffened and broke apart with tiny,
mewling gasps that would have sent him over the edge
if he hadn't already been sporting granite in his pants,
full and thick, ready for action.

He was more than ready to sink into that slick heat,
but he wanted to make sure she got hers first, because

as he'd admitted to Alexis, he was a gentleman at heart even if he had the mind of a lecherous pervert.

Layton gave her clitoris one final tease and she jerked, her belly spasming involuntarily. "You're a bad boy," she said with a satisfied grin. "And I like it. Do you always let ladies come first?"

"Seems a good rule to live by," he said, rising to seal his lips to hers, loving that she gripped him hard and didn't shy away from the fact that she could taste herself on his lips. He pulled away and Alexis helped him out of his underwear, revealing his thick and eager erection. He grinned and palmed himself. Now he didn't mind that he was naked. "Like what you see?"

"Not bad," she said coyly. "But let's reserve judgment until after it's over. You know what they say about guys with talented tongues…"

"They're lucky bastards?"

She laughed. "They say they're good with their mouths because that's all they got."

Layton laughed and pulled her gently off the sofa, lifting her into his arms. "Honey, I guess I'm the exception. We'll see if you can handle this action."

She smelled like sex and he liked it. "I like the feel of your wet pussy against my arm. Reminds me of where I've been."

"You have a dirty mind," she said with sly approval. "I like the way you think."

"I think we have a lot in common." He placed her on the bed and gazed at the perfection wrapped up in one saucy package. "How is it that I've never met you until this point? Your brother was smart to hide you away."

She snorted. "You make me sound like a virginal princess in the medieval days."

"I'm just saying…if you were my sister I wouldn't want the guys at the station house seeing you, either. You have no idea what a bunch of guys cooped up together start to talk about. It's raunchy."

"Do tell."

"How about I show you?"

She shivered with open delight. "Do your worst."

"Well, sometimes when there are no calls and the station is otherwise dead, we try and one-up each other with tales of sexual adventures."

"Okay, now I'm intrigued. What's the kinkiest place you've had sex?" she asked, scooting onto the pillow and leaning back, giving him the best view of everything she had to offer.

"Easy. Bathroom of the Lotus. She had to cover her mouth to muffle the screams as I banged her hard up against the bathroom wall."

"The Lotus…are you saying you had sex in the swankiest restaurant in town…the same place that takes weeks to get a reservation unless you're a celebrity?"

"As it happened…I was with a certain up-and-coming starlet who I'd met on the slopes in Vail. We hit it off and saw each other a few times until her schedule got too hectic and we lost touch."

"Who was it?"

"I don't kiss and tell."

"You're lying," she said, calling his bluff.

"No, I swear to you. True story. She was a hot lay,"

he admitted as he climbed onto the bed. "But enough about her... I'm all about you right now."

"Good answer," she said, pulling him to her for another kiss, their tongues sparring with one another in a sensual assault. She was good with her mouth. He could only imagine what she'd do with that mouth on his cock, but he couldn't wait for more foreplay. He was willing to forgo a little head if it meant he could sink into that sweet pussy.

But first... "Condoms?"

"First drawer, full box."

"I love a woman who's prepared," he said, jerking open the drawer. He ripped open a foil packet and sheathed himself, his hands shaking. Damn, he was never this eager, but there was something about Alexis that turned him on his ear. So much for the suave act he usually had down to an art form.

Pulling her injured leg up over his shoulder, he slid himself into her damp heat and nearly lost his mind from the instant pleasure cocooning him from all sides. She gripped him with her internal muscles, squeezing him from the inside, and he nearly came like a prepubescent boy in a circle jerk.

"Oh my God," he breathed, unable to stop from uttering a guttural moan. Sweat popped along his hairline. He wanted to pump into her like a piston, to ram his cock into her with the force of a machine, to put his stamp on her insides, and the ferocity of his need shocked and embarrassed him a little. "You feel so good," he admitted with a tight groan.

He drove into Alexis, burying himself to the hilt, losing all sense of cool as he thrust against her. Remembering some semblance of himself, he slowed his thrusts to focus on her, loving the way her cheeks flushed with each moan as her generous breasts bounced with the motion of his hips, everything about her was sexy.

Within moments, she was tensing and her thighs shaking and he knew she was close, which was a blessed relief because he didn't think he could last much longer. He liked to pride himself on being able to go the distance, but something about Alexis stripped him bare and made him vulnerable at the same time.

All he wanted was to lose himself in her, to watch as she came and to taste her on his tongue. He wanted to bury his face in her pussy and lap at her folds until she cried out his name. He'd never been one to wax poetic about a woman's lady parts, but he thought he could write a sonnet about the sweetness that was Alexis.

"L-Layton!" she cried out, gripping the pillow beneath her head, thrusting her breasts up as she came hard. She shuddered and a long exhale escaped her lips as she completely lost herself to the moment. It was beautiful to watch and almost interrupted his own orgasm, but within seconds of that undoing, he followed, coming with a loud groan.

He rolled off and pulled the condom free, tossing it carefully into the trash before collapsing to the bed, spent. It took him several minutes before he could form words, but Alexis didn't seem to mind the silence. If anything, the satisfied smile on her face said more than words could, and that made him want to crow.

"I needed that," she said with a happy sigh. "Thank you."

He paused and then nodded. "You're welcome."

A happy gurgle of satisfaction escaped her sweet lips and he wanted her all over again. Could this become his newest bad habit?

7

LAYTON ROLLED ONTO his side. "If you're this good in bed laid up, I can only imagine what it's like being with you when you're fully recovered."

She leveled a playful look his way. "I like to switch positions. A lot."

"Sex is great cardio. Best way to work up a sweat in my book. Should I stock up on Gatorade?"

She laughed. "Getting ahead of yourself, don't you think?"

"Not really. I think we both had a good time. Am I wrong?"

"Oh no, you were good, no doubt about that. I rarely come that easily, so I either chalk that up to the fact that you're pretty talented or I was pretty horny. Either way, I count that as a win."

"I think it's because I'm pretty talented," Layton said with cocky swagger. "I don't mean to brag, but... I'm pretty good."

Alexis made a show of thinking then decided. "Sorry, buddy, I think I was just really horny and needed an itch scratched. Thanks for that, by the way," she repeated.

He laughed, reaching for her. "All right, not sure who's winning this argument because I feel as if I'm coming out the winner either way, so let's call it a draw and proceed with funky times."

Alexis pealed with laughter. "Funky times? That sounds like something that needs an antibiotic."

He kissed her and she enjoyed the feel of his lips against hers, but after a long moment of wrangling tongues, she gently pulled away, leaving him perplexed.

"What's wrong?"

"I just want to be clear about what we're doing."

He grinned. "Isn't it obvious?"

She pushed at him, needing him to be serious for a minute. "No, I mean, I want to make sure that we're both okay with the agreement that this is just for today."

The sweet warmth in Layton's dark eyes faded and she suffered a twinge of guilt, but they both knew they couldn't mess around once Erik returned. For one, Alexis would never come between Erik and his good friend and, two, Alexis didn't think she was ready to start seriously dating again. She still had…*issues* she was working through about her breakup with Riker and it wasn't fair to Layton to drag him down that dark road.

"Kind of a downer conversation after such a great start," he said.

"Agreed, but one that needs to be had, right?"

He sighed. "Yeah," he said, but he looked as if having this conversation wasn't high on his priority list. "Still a bummer."

"Can we be friends after this?" she asked.

"We're not friends," he reminded her. "We just met."

"And what better way to build a great friendship than letting our naked parts rub up against one another. I had an anthropology instructor once tell me that everyone should use sex to defuse conflict, like the bonobo monkeys. Any time they are confused or conflicted, they bang it out and, voilà, everyone is happy again."

"If only things were so easily resolved," he said wryly, plainly not impressed or on board with her suggestion to keep things platonic going forward.

"You seem irritated," she said. "Are you mad?"

"No, not mad. I get where you're coming from. Just feels weird to be on the other side of that argument."

"Aw, how cute," she crooned with a laugh, and he broke a small grin. "But I'm really serious about not getting involved with anyone until I have my degree in my hot little hand. You have no idea how it feels to be the one that everyone writes off. I'm not saying it wasn't my fault and that I didn't make things worse with my choices, but it still sucks."

"Your brother adores you," Layton said with a mild frown. "And he's proud of you. He's told me so."

"Really?"

"Yeah, really. The only thing he's ever said that was remotely negative had everything to do with that douche you were dating. Erik didn't like him."

No, Erik hadn't thought much of Riker. Neither had

her dad, now that she thought about it, but she'd been too head over heels in love to see the warning signs. "I wish I'd listened to them in the first place and dumped him," she admitted.

"Hey, don't be so hard on yourself. You know that saying, you have to kiss a lot of frogs before you find Prince Charming? Well, I think that's applicable here."

A warm smile found Alexis's lips. "So full of wisdom, aren't you?"

"Only because I've made my share of dumb moves and I have the scars to prove it."

She tucked her robe around her. "I would've thought that this would've been a convenient out for you. Not many guys would find a weekend fling outside of their wheelhouse."

"I didn't say it was outside of my wheelhouse. I've done it before," he corrected with a shrug. "I just didn't think you'd be okay with a one-and-done."

"I'm not…but a day of sex with you sounds just about perfect."

"You sure about that?" he asked, his dark eyes threatening to drown her in their beautiful depths. And those eyelashes! Criminal!

She hadn't lied when she'd said she'd come faster with Layton than anyone else and it'd been a pretty fantastic orgasm—not like some weak little tingle that barely registered but one of those earth-shattering oh-my-God-was-that-real kind of things and that was hard to give up, but she was determined to stay the course. "Yep," she said with more force. "Now, I'm going to bake cookies. You can help if you want."

"Cookies? Why now?"

"Because it's part of my holiday tradition, just like hanging the lights, and keeping to my schedule is one way to stay on track with my goals."

The fact that I'm already thinking of you in ways I shouldn't is enough of a warning sign. Yep, so go bake cookies, Alexis!

And then she left him in her bedroom.

HUMMING UNDER HER BREATH, Alexis hobbled to the kitchen, determined to bake some gingerbread cookies before Erik returned. Erik was a sucker for her cookies and Alexis was not above using his love for cookies to get what she wanted, such as premium cable when Erik had been adamant that it was a useless expense. Erik was far more frugal than her—hence the belief by their parents that he was the more responsible one.

Well, that and the fact that he seemed to have his life on track whereas she had made more than a few stops and starts.

Such as when she agreed to let an internet start-up company slap their logo all over her car with the promise of paying her rent for six months when, in fact, the company had gone belly up within a month and she'd been left with a hideous logo blazoned across her bumper, which had to be professionally removed at her own cost.

In hindsight, she should've known that any company named Jiggity, with the tagline *The jig is up!* wasn't going to last.

And then there was, of course, her experience with Riker that certainly rose to the top of the pile.

And now that she'd shagged Erik's best friend, Alexis thought it might be prudent to have some tasty yumminess around the house to soften the blow, if he were to somehow find out, which she was going to do her best to ensure that he didn't. But a girl should always have a Plan B, right?

Too bad she hadn't had a Plan B with Riker.

Ugh. What had she been thinking? She had to stop being swayed by a hot body and a bad-boy attitude. Bad boys didn't hold down solid jobs, and they spent your money and slept with your former sorority sisters.

She set the cookie tin down with more force than necessary just as Layton joined her in the kitchen. Alexis hit him with a blinding smile and began chattering as if they hadn't just spent time in each other's arms because, frankly, she needed to put her mind on a different track.

"So, tell me about yourself," she started, grabbing the ingredients for the cookies and the mixing bowls. "What's it like to play the hero all day?"

"I wish it were that simple. Being a firefighter isn't saving kittens and rescuing damsels from fiery buildings all day. Sometimes, on slow days, it's scrubbing a station toilet that's been used by twelve other guys."

She wrinkled her nose. "That sounds like punishment."

"Let's just say, some of my station brethren aren't as diligent about hitting the pot."

"I would murder someone," Alexis said, biting back a laugh. "I mean, that's really gross."

"Yes, it is."

"Tell me more about this unglamorous side of being

a firefighter," she said as she worked the dough, loving the smell of fresh cookie dough. In a past life, she was a French baker, she was sure of it.

"You really want to know?"

"Sure. We've got time to kill."

"I can think of other ways to kill time," he suggested, walking over to her. Her hands were stuck in dough, trapped in the sticky glob, and he took delightful advantage. His lips brushed across hers and she melted a little. "Are you sure you want to talk about station life?" he murmured against her lips.

"No fair," she said with a breathy little sigh. "You are one of the best kissers I've ever had the privilege of kissing."

He grinned and kissed her again. He swallowed her moan and she accidentally put too much pressure on her sore ankle, causing her to yelp and pull back. "Ouch. Sorry," she said, lifting her foot. "Still tender."

"You shouldn't be on it," he reminded her. "It won't heal if you don't let the swelling go down."

He surprised her by lifting her up on the counter, spreading her legs to stand between them. She automatically looped her arms around his neck. "See? Isn't that better?" he asked.

"Of course it is," she agreed with a laugh. "But you're messing with my plans."

"Make new ones," he murmured right before sealing his mouth to hers, stealing her breath and for a moment, her will to be a good girl. But this—*this exact thing!*—was the reason she kept making the wrong decisions in her life.

Alexis reluctantly pulled away. "I really need to get these cookies done."

"Please tell me that's a unique euphemism for getting it on in the kitchen."

She laughed and pushed him away so she could slide from the counter. "Sorry, bud. Not this time. You'll just have to shelve your dirty mind for a minute."

He groaned as if that were impossible and she wanted to say, *I feel your pain*, but she didn't want to make things harder—ha! No pun intended—than they already were in the *hands-off* department.

She cast a playful scowl his way. "Don't get in the way of my baking. You don't want to see me when someone has blocked my cookie habit."

He raised his hands in mock surrender. "Far be it from me to prevent the lady from whipping up something delicious and sweet."

Alexis grinned and returned to her dough, which was just about ready. She grabbed the rolling pin and began rolling out the dough. "Do you like gingerbread cookies?" she asked.

"Not really."

She did a double take. "What?"

"Sorry. I don't care for the taste of molasses."

"Well, you've plainly never experienced a good gingerbread cookie, which you will once you eat mine."

"I'm willing to be wowed, but you ought to temper your expectations, just in case."

"Never."

He laughed. "Okay," he conceded and then added, "You asked about unglamorous station life? Well, it's like this… When things are slow, we're out mowing the grass, washing the trucks, doing outreach at the schools and renewing our certifications. Like I said, totally unglamorous."

"Well, it beats being a perpetual student," Alexis admitted. "I'm ready to be done."

"You're smart going all the way. Being at the top of the food chain is a good thing."

Alexis appreciated his vote, even if they were going to keep things casual. "I wish you weren't my brother's buddy," she said, mostly under her breath, but it was a titch louder than she'd meant it to be. She risked a glance at Layton and he seemed to understand her comment.

"You're the one making the rules," he said by way of saying, *Hey, things can be different if you want them to be,* but she knew better than to give in to that flimsy hope. Layton read her mind and added, "I think Erik would be cool."

She chuckled. "No, he most definitely wouldn't be cool about you and me. He's very protective, especially of late. It feels good that he cares, but it does get a little tiresome when he treats me like a kid."

"Older-brother gig. Occupational hazard."

"Yeah, I guess so. Anyway—" she cast a wry look at Layton "—he won't be chill about his best buddy shacking up with his little sister, and I would never want to come between you and Erik."

"I can handle Erik," Layton returned stubbornly, and in that moment she believed him, but she didn't want Erik and Layton going to blows just because she'd practically seduced Layton and now they both wanted more. "Besides, you're an adult. He has to come to grips with the fact that you're capable of making your own decisions, good *and* bad."

"True, but it's probably not a good idea to shove it in his face."

Layton leaned in. Her breath caught and, for the life of her, she couldn't speak. His big, rough hands gripped her ass and pulled her to him. Their parts fit together so perfectly it was almost a sin not to allow them to interlock. His tab was aligned exquisitely with her slot and she almost giggled at the ridiculous bent of her thoughts only because laughter was her defense mechanism when she was nervous.

"Here's the way I see it," he said in a seductively low voice, "for whatever reasons, we mesh pretty good. Unless I was mistaken and you're the world's best actress, you were having a pretty good time, too. The cat is out of the bag, babe. Can't stuff that genie back in the bottle now."

"I get the idea," she said, lifting her chin and meeting his gaze. "Doesn't mean I'm willing to put a wedge between you and my brother just because epically good sex is on the line."

He gently backed her against the counter. "Are you sure about that?"

"Positive," she said with a breathy tone that even to her own ears sounded like a come-on. But before she could try again and set him straight, he turned her around and she was bent over the counter and his hand was up her robe, squeezing her bare ass. "What are you doing?" she asked, biting her lip to keep from smiling. She knew she ought to stop him but she'd always been a sucker for a good time and a bad idea. "The cookies!"

"Screw the cookies," he said with a growl as the sound of foil tearing made her turn and she gasped when she saw him sheathing himself in a fresh condom. He'd brought it with him out of the bedroom. Kudos for thinking ahead, but she really ought to give him hell for being presumptuous. Except she was lifting her ass, closing her eyes against the inevitable sensation of his cock pressing past her folds, going in deep, and she couldn't wait.

"Do it then," she said, eager to feel him again, even though she'd just made a big show of saying they should forget it ever happened. Okay, maybe just one more time and then she'd really put her foot down.

And then, as if he'd read her mind, he didn't waste time sliding inside her, pushing hard and hitting that sweet spot with unerring accuracy when most guys had to have a little direction. She groaned like a cat in heat, losing herself in the pleasure of being bent over, taken and used mercilessly. It worked for her, and the fact that Layton seemed to appreciate that hidden part of her was an even bigger turn-on.

Riker had always made her feel bad for expressing her needs, but then he'd cheated on her with every woman who happened to twitch her hips at him, which had only served to do a number on her self-esteem.

But right now, Riker was the last person she wanted to think about. Layton was doing her right and that was all that mattered.

Maybe those monkeys were onto something. Sex was certainly working to alleviate her stress!

This time wasn't as quick, but that served them both well. Layton took his time to really give it to her good, alternating slow and hard thrusts with fast piston action. She couldn't catch her breath, but it was so good all she could do was hang on for dear life as he pounded her with the single-minded attention of a man on a mission.

God, she loved a man with purpose. Just when she thought she might scream from the building pressure, she burst and wondrous explosions of pleasure blasted her nerve endings, squeezing her muscles and sending her into orbit. She didn't notice the pain in her ankle or the granite counter grinding against her hips, only sweet, sweet oblivion.

"God, yes, Alexis," he gasped, gripping her hips as he pushed into her, coming hard as he pumped erratically, all semblance of finesse out the window. She loved that he lost control with her, that he couldn't seem to get a handle on his game. She didn't want to be the only one losing all sense of reason and cool.

He shuddered and his grip fell away from her hips, even as he remained firmly inside her. She pulsed with residual spasms as her orgasm slowly receded. She didn't remember the sex being this good with Riker. Surely that was just the mind playing tricks with the memory because she'd discovered Riker was a dick? It couldn't be that she and Layton, of all people, had some serious sexual connection that they were both slave to?

He withdrew and removed the condom, tossing it in the trash and then, without a word, scooped her up and carried her to the sofa.

"What are you doing?" she asked, amused that he always felt compelled to carry her. It was sexy and made her feel distinctly feminine, even if it embarrassed her a little because she could still walk.

"Movie time," he said, leaving and returning with Erik's robe and slipping it on.

Alexis gasped and then laughed. "Erik will kill you if he finds out you're wearing his favorite robe."

"Wearing his robe is the least of my offenses today."

"That's true," she acknowledged, admiring how sexy he looked in nothing but a robe. They were like a couple, spending the weekend together—except they weren't a couple and never would be. The jarring thought dampened her enthusiasm for a minute but if all they had was this weekend, she supposed they might as well do it right. "You really want to watch a movie? Why can't we just spend all weekend screwing each other's brains out?"

"As much as I'm down with that, a man needs a little recovery time. We also need to fit in a shower at some point because we might start to smell."

She laughed, loving how easy it was to hang out with Layton but soon enough the jab of reality was too much to ignore. "You know we can't just pretend that whatever this is will work out in the end because it won't."

Layton regarded her with a slight smile. "Are you an all-or-nothing kind of girl?"

Alexis stopped to think. "Maybe. I don't know. I don't know what kind of girl I am right now. Riker messed with my head in a big way. I thought I was in love with him. Finding out that the man you imagined building a life with is a douche kinda throws you into a tailspin."

"I hear ya," he agreed easily. "I thought Julianne was the one until I found out she was screwing her boss. I'd say that threw me for a loop."

"How'd you find out?" she asked, intrigued. It was somehow soothing to commiserate with someone else who'd been equally screwed over by their ex. "Was it like something out of a movie?"

"Nothing so dramatic, actually. I didn't bust in on them during one of their trysts. I found a text message."

"That must've been a pretty incriminating text message."

"No, not terribly, but I sensed there was something off about it and I just asked her point-blank if she was screwing the guy. She caved pretty quickly and admitted it. Told me she'd been trying to break it off with me for months but I was such a good guy she didn't want to hurt me. And you know what, when she said that, I was feeling pretty much the opposite of a good guy because of the things I wanted to say to her, but I didn't say shit. I just packed my things and told her to have a nice life."

"You let her off easy," Alexis said, remembering her own showdown with Riker. She was embarrassed to admit she'd gone a little loco. "I keyed Riker's truck. Actually, I carved *cheater* into the hood. It's going to cost him a bundle to fix that."

Layton whistled low. "Damn, girl, you went after the man's truck? That's cold."

"No, what was cold was catching him jerking off in

the middle of the night on his webcam to my former sorority sister. He thought I was asleep and I caught him with his pants down. Literally. Actually, it turned my stomach. I couldn't believe he would do something so low. But after that, I discovered that wasn't the first, and probably wouldn't be the last, time he cheated on me, so I bailed."

"After leaving him a lovely parting gift," he supplied helpfully, and Alexis nodded. "Sounds appropriate."

"I thought it was."

He chuckled and they shared a quiet moment together. It was weird to share something so incredibly painful with a virtual stranger and yet feel relieved to let it go. Not even Erik knew the full details. At the time, Alexis had been too embarrassed to share the nitty-gritty, choosing instead to say Riker had cheated and leave it at that.

"So, after Julianne, you jumped into the dating pool?"

"Yeah, probably too soon. A buddy told me the best way to get over a woman was to find another one right away. I wasn't sure that was the best advice, but I was hurting and desperate to feel better, so I went on a dating spree that mostly turned into a blur of sexual mishaps, one-night stands and unfortunate mistakes that I knew I had to stop or else I'd never stand a chance of respecting myself again."

Compassion softened her voice as she said, "You know, I get it...the need to feel good after hurting so bad. I went the slutty route for a little while, but when I realized that it wasn't making me feel better I invested in a good vibrator and stopped chasing dicks."

"What kind of vibrator?"

She pushed at his shoulder with mock indignation. "You never ask a lady about her toys. That's private."

"Is it bad that I would give my right nut to watch you pleasure yourself?"

Now she gasped for real and the blush heating her cheeks could warm a small country, but the fact that he wanted to watch her turned her on in a big way. "Are you a voyeur?" she ventured, curious.

"With you, I think I'd be anything you wanted me to be."

"Stop it," she said, his openness tickling her. "You're making me blush and you're playing me like a fiddle."

"I don't know what it is about you, but everything I've said is true. You're different, Alexis. I don't know why and, trust me, I wish I could figure it out so I could put the kibosh on it. I get it, we are complicating everything, but I can't seem to stop and I don't want to. You turn my crank in the hottest way, and that's saying a lot."

What could she say in the face of such brutal honesty? It was a breath of fresh air after everything she'd been through with Riker. He was a born liar. The words that'd popped from his mouth were always peppered with half truths, a fact she'd only discovered after she'd been thoroughly humiliated. "Julianne was an idiot," she murmured, shooting him a quick look. "If she didn't see what a good guy you are… She was blind."

"Same goes for Riker. I can't imagine letting someone like you go."

"What is happening between us? This can't be natural, right?"

"We have insane sexual chemistry," he agreed, equally mystified. "I wonder what would've happened if we'd met before we both were burned."

"I wouldn't have been attracted to you."

He did a double take. "Come again?"

She soothed his ego. "It's not you. It's me. Honestly, what attracted me to Riker was his bad-boy attitude and the fact that he drove a motorcycle. I wouldn't have been attracted to you because you have a good job and you're a decent guy."

Layton relaxed and laughed. "Yeah, well, I know I would've looked twice your way. You have the kind of breasts I dream about."

Alexis giggled, loving how free he was with compliments. "Did Julianne have big boobs, too?"

"Yeah, but I gotta say, and I'm not just saying this because we hooked up, but your breasts…damn… they're so awesome."

He grinned then added, "However, hindsight being what it is, I've since realized that I couldn't marry a woman that didn't stimulate me intellectually."

"I know what you mean. Riker was smart but in an arrogant way. He enjoyed one-upping people. It was embarrassing at times."

"He sounds like a peach."

"A rotten one."

"There is that." He shifted and as he did, the robe gaped, and she got an unobstructed view of his cock, lying semi-erect against his thigh. He tracked her gaze and grinned, allowing the robe to open farther. "See something you like?"

"I can't believe you're getting hard again. You have the stamina of a horse."

"Not always. I'm telling you…it's you."

He'd been so giving thus far, going down on her, making sure she came first. Riker had been an inordinately selfish lover, almost never seeing to her needs first. God, why had she stayed with him as long as she had? Sliding her robe down, she bared her breasts for Layton's gaze. Interest flared in his eyes and his cock sprang to life as if given a shot of Viagra. She couldn't help but laugh. "That's a cool party trick in some circles."

Layton grinned and she was struck by how damn adorable he was. Sure, he was sexy, that was a given, but how had she missed just how sweet and cute he was? And he deserved a little selfish loving. She leaned over and slipped his cock in her mouth, delighting in the way his hand automatically went to her hair and stroked her head lightly as she sucked him. His cock held the faint taste of latex but she didn't mind. Soon enough his touch became more urgent as she worked his cock, using her hands and tongue to tease him to his breaking point without pushing him over. She took him to the edge several times until he was practically begging her for release and then, because her jaw was getting tired, she allowed him to come.

Layton groaned as he spurted his load down her throat and she gulped greedily, wanting to know his taste just as he'd eagerly acquainted himself with hers.

He gripped the sofa cushion as he lost control, shouting her name as he came—and that was hotter than hot.

She wasn't sure how she was going to quit Layton Davis.

In record time, he'd just become her most wicked secret vice.

8

THE STORM ARRIVED by midafternoon but by that time Alexis and Layton were quite comfortable to ride it out snuggled with each other. They'd even managed to bake a batch of cookies in between some serious fooling around—several orgasms—and a shower later.

"You know, I expected to hear from Emma and Erik by now," Alexis said, feeling slightly guilty for not even thinking about her brother and best friend until that moment. She grabbed her cell and quickly called. It rang twice and then went to voice mail. She frowned. "That's odd. Em never turns off her phone. She's addicted to it."

"They're probably in a bad service area," Layton said. "I wouldn't worry. Erik will take good care of Emma."

"I know he will." She settled on the sofa with the popcorn she'd just popped. "Want to know a secret?"

"Sure," he answered, grabbing a handful.

"Emma has always had a raging crush on Erik since

we were kids. She thinks I never noticed but it was plainly obvious."

"How'd you know?"

"Well, for one, girls always know when a girl likes a guy. Second, it was easy to catch her mooning over him, staring at him like a starving puppy whenever he was around. It was really annoying, actually."

"So, has Erik ever shown an interest in Emma?"

"God no. And I'm glad for that! How weird would that be to have my best friend shacking up with my brother? I can't handle the imagery."

"It's no weirder than what we're doing," he reminded her.

"No, it's totally different."

"How so?"

"Because it is." She left it at that. There was no way he could convince her that the situations were similar because she didn't want them to be similar. "Besides, Emma and Erik are complete opposites. They'd never suit."

"Your brother is a good guy. Why wouldn't you want your best friend to find a man worth her time?"

"Oh, come on, don't throw sensible arguments my way. I think we've already established logic and reason have no bearing on my decision-making process. They aren't good together—end of story."

He laughed and tossed back some kernels. "You're a hypocrite."

"Am not."

"You are. But you're still cute so I forgive you."

"I am not a hypocrite. I just…ugh. I can't stomach

the idea of my brother getting jiggy with my best friend since grammar school. Is that so wrong?"

"It's a little selfish," he said with a shrug.

Alexis gasped. "You don't know me well enough to pass judgment."

"Maybe not, but it seems to me that you'd want your best friend to end up with a good guy. I'm surprised you haven't tried to hook them up."

Alexis frowned. Emma and Erik? It made her feel squicky. "Erik looks at Emma like a kid sister."

"Not the way I saw him looking at her."

"What do you mean?" Alexis stared hard at Layton, wondering what the heck he was talking about. "Erik thinks of Emma like a sister," she repeated, stubbornly refusing to believe that her brother was thinking of Emma in any other way besides brotherly.

"Look, it's not a big deal, but I think Erik was seeing that Emma was all grown up. I mean, she's hot. I can't blame him for looking."

Alexis glared, feeling a tad bit jealous, and she had no right to. "I know what my friend looks like."

Layton leaned forward and surprised her with a kiss. "Calm down, tigress. Emma's not my type."

"And I wouldn't care if she was," she quipped a little too quickly. Her heart rate had kicked up a notch and she realized she was being ridiculous. "Okay, I'm a little reluctant to admit that you may have a point. But there's no sense in worrying over something that hasn't happened, right?"

"Right," he agreed. "But I know what I saw."

"You *think* you know what you saw," she returned

stubbornly. "But in the meantime, I just want Emma to call so I know they're all right."

Layton nodded with understanding. "So, where are your parents this holiday?"

"Scotland," she answered with a sigh. "Something about checking off items on their bucket list before they die. I think my mom just didn't want to host Christmas dinner and this was a convenient way to get out of it."

"Scotland is pretty far to travel to get out of dinner."

"You don't know my mom," she said dryly. "She's not your average-mom type."

"How's your foot?"

She slowly rotated it. "Not bad. It feels much better. Just a small twinge."

"That's good. You should still baby it though."

"Yes, Doctor."

His gaze turned playful. "I'll play doctor if you'll be the naughty nurse."

Alexis tossed a popcorn kernel at him with a grin. "And that is not happening, so lose that idea. If anything, I'll be the doctor and you can be the naughty nurse."

"Intriguing. I'm secure enough in my manhood to try a little power exchange. Are we talking spankings and bondage? Be gentle, I'm a beginner." She barked a shocked laugh and he tackled her to the sofa cushion to kiss her hard and fast. "You're just full of surprises, Alexis Matheson," he said, pulling away.

"That was not an invitation to go buy whips and chains," she joked. "I'm mostly vanilla with a dash of chocolate on top."

"My favorite flavor is vanilla," he said, smiling. "So that's fine with me."

She sobered. "What are we doing?"

"Whatever we want," he answered.

"Will it be weird to see each other socially like nothing happened?"

"Yes."

She frowned then groaned. "I wish you would lie to me a little."

"No you don't."

"You're right. I hate liars."

He brushed a soft kiss across her lips. "I don't know what's in store, all I know is that right now you are the center of my universe, the storm is going to knock out the power at some point and all I care about is spending whatever available moment with you. I'm not even thinking beyond this weekend."

"Me neither," she admitted, looping her arms around his neck. "Is it bad that I don't want to think about tomorrow?"

"If it's bad, I'm right there with you."

"It's strange, don't you think, that we have this connection? I've never felt so comfortable with another person I just met, especially a guy."

"I can't explain it, either. Maybe it's fate."

"Do you believe in fate?"

He hedged with a guilty smile. "Not exactly, but I am a closet romantic and I like the idea that fate exists."

"Me, too."

Too bad it wasn't as black-and-white as *I like you, you like me*. Erik had always been her champion, always seeing the best in her. How would he react to knowing that she'd gleefully seduced his best friend? She couldn't stand the idea of suffering Erik's disappointment in her behavior. She should've kept her hands to herself and just white-knuckled her attraction to Layton.

But even as she knew they'd both jumped feet first into the pool without caring if there was water beneath them, a part of her wasn't sorry and maybe that was a problem.

Maybe the worst part was knowing she'd do it again.

LAYTON KNEW HE was playing with fire, but the more time he spent with Alexis the more he wanted. He had an insatiable need to know her more deeply, to touch and feel, and he was a little disconcerted by how easy they slipped into an effortless familiarity with one another. Would they be able to pull off a nonchalance among other people? Erik would know right away. Hell, maybe he ought to just spill his guts and hope for mercy.

He sat up and pulled Alexis with him. "How's this for an idea…let's just tell Erik that we hooked up and let the chips fall where they may."

"That would go over like a lead balloon. I don't recommend it."

Clearly, Alexis didn't find as much merit in the idea as he did. "Don't you think Erik would respect our decision to come to him instead of letting him find out by accident?"

"No. A big fat no. My brother is very protective of

me, and ever since I broke up with Riker, he's been superprotective."

"I'm not like Riker," he pointed out, trying not to suffer a ruffled ego at any accidental comparisons. "And your brother knows I'm not a bad guy."

"Of course not but just because he thinks you're a swell guy to go fishing with doesn't mean he wants you hooking up with his little sister. Besides, what's the point of sharing? We're not planning to be a couple anytime soon, so why rock the boat unnecessarily."

Ah, there was the heart of the matter, right? Maybe he wanted to explore the possibility of a relationship with Alexis. But did she want that? He decided to test the waters. "And what if that changed?"

"What if what changed?" she asked, confused.

"What if…we wanted to try out a relationship?"

For a split second he caught a sliver of yearning in her gaze, as if she might like to try a relationship on for size, but she shut it down quickly. "You know that's not going to work between us. Let me just tell you… I'm a mess right now. I'm smashed against deadlines, midterms, impossible classloads and I'm moody as hell, to boot. I am not girlfriend material."

"Usually people list the pro points instead of just jumping straight to the con list."

"Yeah, well, maybe if more people were starkly honest there'd be a whole helluva lot less heartache. I think people should just put it all out on the table and let people decide if it's something they can handle. I mean, I wish Riker had admitted to me on our first date that he was a serial cheater without a loyal or faithful bone in his body because then I could've decided right then and there that I didn't want to take that on. But instead, I had to find out the hard—and painful—way." She drew a deep breath before asking, "Don't you think you would've liked to know that Julianne was a cheater before you took a chance on her?"

"Sure. But love is a risk. Even if I had known up front she had a wandering eye, I'm not sure I would've done anything differently."

"Yeah, well, I'm telling you right now… I'm a bad investment."

Layton heard the pain in her voice, hidden beneath the false bravado, and it struck him that she was scared of being hurt again. That's what it was all about for them both, right? Maybe that was the connection drawing them, which meant eventually such a flimsy connection would fade. Rebound relationships were transient for a reason.

"Okay," he accepted her reasoning with a small nod. "I guess you make a good point. We'll keep our weekend to ourselves and I'll do my best to pretend that I don't know what you sound like when you come." She sucked in a wild breath and he grinned. "Sorry?"

"You're not sorry. You did that on purpose."

"Guilty."

She allowed a small smile and he wanted to kiss away whatever was making her secretly sad. She regarded him with those beautiful, soulful eyes that snapped with mischief most times but right now were filled with wells of yearning that seemed so deep he might drown. He ran a knuckle down her soft cheek.

"Circumstances change us but they don't have to

ruin us," he reminded her gently. "Don't let one ass-hole destroy the part of you that's precious."

"Easier said than done," Alexis said with a forlorn sigh. "Most times I just feel so incredibly stupid for letting him into my heart when he clearly didn't be-long there."

"It's all just a rehearsal until the curtain goes up on opening night, babe. That dick was just a bit player in your show."

She smiled wider. "Got some theater in your back-ground?"

"Father was a drama teacher at my local high school," he admitted with a short grin. "Can't seem to help myself. They're the only metaphors I seem to remember."

"I like it," Alexis said, slowly losing the sadness. "It's kinda profound. Made me think of things in a different way."

"My dad will be happy to know that his words live on."

Alexis grabbed his hand and pulled him from the sofa, leading him to the bedroom.

"I seem to remember someone wanting to watch…"

Layton nearly swallowed his tongue.

And just like that, Alexis managed to turn on a dime from broken butterfly, struggling to fly, to sexy temptress ready to eat him alive, and the contradic-tion was a wild turn-on.

Hell, everything she did turned him on!

How was he going to get Alexis out of his system when the weekend was done?

Something told him Alexis was in his blood—and there was nothing he could do about it.

Funny thing…he was okay with that.

9

THE FOLLOWING MORNING Alexis woke up to the stillness of fresh snow outside the window and Layton curled around her as if it was his natural place to be and for an instant she just savored the moment.

It couldn't last, but that didn't mean she couldn't enjoy every second until it was over.

But even as she was snuggled against his solid warmth, she was troubled by the fact that neither Erik nor Emma had called to check in yet.

Erik was a stickler for calling when he reached his destination. As a first responder, he'd seen too many tragic accidents to not call. The fact that she knew that about her brother only served to make her more nervous.

Layton stirred and his hand found her breast, causing her to smile briefly. Man, he wasn't joking about being a boob man.

"Morning," he murmured, his breath tickling her neck. "You talk in your sleep."

"I know. Did I say anything interesting?"

"Nothing that I could make out. It was mostly gibberish."

"Did I keep you awake?"

"Nope. As soon as I realized you were out like a light and just talking in your sleep, I went right back to sleep."

She smiled, happy to be in bed with him, but soon enough she remembered her concern about Emma and Erik and voiced them. "You know, I'm really stressed that Erik and Emma haven't checked in. It's not like Erik to go radio silence."

"They probably got in late and didn't want to wake you."

She shook her head. "No, Erik always calls. It's sort of an OCD thing. He wouldn't have been able to sleep without letting me know that they were okay."

Layton rose on his elbow and she rolled to her back to gaze at him. He frowned. "I'm sure there's a logical explanation, but I understand your concern. Erik is pretty consistent in his habits."

"And Emma would call, too. She's a worrywart by nature and she'd never forget to call because she wouldn't want me to worry."

"Well, we can call the road patrol and see if there were any accidents," he suggested and she shivered at the thought. "It might, if nothing else, ease your mind."

"Or it could send me into a panic if it turns out they're not okay."

"Let's not jump to the worst-case scenario," he said, kissing her softly and instantly soothing her nerves. "Breakfast first and then we'll figure out what's going on with your brother and Emma."

"You're such a good guy," she gushed, wrapping

her arms around his neck. "Tell me again why I don't want to keep you forever?"

"Because according to you, you're a bad girlfriend," he supplied, tongue in cheek. "But I think it's because you don't want to be tied down with someone like me who's serially monogamous."

She made a face to hide the sudden racing of her heart rate. Was he right? Was she afraid of trusting again? *Possibly.* "That was the most passive-aggressive statement I've ever heard so early in the morning," she said with a small roll of her eyes. The best defense was a good offense.

But Layton wasn't giving up. "Fair enough. How's this? Because you're afraid I'm going to be clumsy with your heart like that last douche even though we're nothing alike."

Oh, he hit the nail on the head. "No one ever starts out acting badly," she told him quietly, hating that she was still affected by what Riker had done. It was hard to think of yourself as a strong, independent woman when you were still licking the wounds from the past. "That comes later."

"Only if you're hardwired that way from the start." He kissed her—perhaps to stop her from thinking too much—and it worked. Within moments, they were touching, feeling, tasting and loving each other as if the world were about to end.

By the time they emerged from the bedroom, they were starving and raided the kitchen to make French toast and bacon.

"Easiest way to my heart," she admitted around a generous bite of French toast. "I swear I'll be four hundred pounds by the time I'm middle-aged. I love food.

I cringe at the thought of cutting out carbs or going paleo or doing any of those crazy restrictive food plans. I need variety. I need sugar and carbs and grains! I rue the day someone tries to put me on some kind of diet."

"Hey, more meat on your bones means one thing. Bigger boobs, so eat up all you want."

She laughed. "You're impossible. There's more to life than boobs."

"Debatable."

She finished her breakfast and then she grabbed her phone only to find it dead. She'd forgotten to charge it last night and now it was completely dead and it would take about fifteen minutes to even get a tiny signal.

"Can you call Erik and see if he answers? My phone is deader than a doornail."

Layton fished his phone out of his pocket and quickly dialed Erik.

To her relief, Erik picked up.

"Hey, man, there you are," Layton said, gesturing to the phone with a thumbs-up to indicate everything was A-okay. "Your sister was freaking out because you didn't call."

But then Layton sobered and frowned with concern and she knew something was wrong. "What is it?" she asked, tugging at Layton's sleeve. "Is everything okay? What happened?"

He held up his hand to quiet her as he was listening and then said, "All right, that sucks but glad to hear you're okay. That could've ended a lot worse. So you're going to stay there until the car is repaired?"

Car? Her eyes widened. "What happened to the car?"

Layton covered the microphone and whispered, "They were in a minor car accident. The SUV slid

off the road and landed in a ditch but they're okay."
He returned to Erik. "Alexis's foot is fine. The swelling went down and we didn't need to take her to the hospital. I've been taking real good care of her."

At that, Alexis pinched his nipple and he tried not to yelp. "Don't worry about Alexis... I got everything under control." Then his expression changed and he frowned. Something told her Erik was giving him an earful about something he didn't like. "We'll talk more when you get home. Drive safe."

Once he clicked off, Alexis pounced. "What happened?" she demanded to know. "Is everyone okay?"

"They're both fine but it was a little scary. They slid off the road into a ditch and because of the snow no one saw them right away. No injuries, just a little shaken up."

"I knew something was wrong. Erik and Emma are both OCD in that they would've called." She worried her bottom lip. "Poor Em! She just wanted to spend the weekend with her parents and all these terrible mishaps happened. It's almost as if the universe didn't want her to be there. I wonder what that's about."

"Well," Layton said with a small shrug, "if I'm right about Erik seeing Emma as more than just your friend...maybe spending some alone time worked out for them."

She scowled. "There you go again talking about things that make me want to vomit. If you knew Emma, you'd never suggest that she'd have sex in a vehicle. She's very shy."

"The right man, the right circumstances can bring out hidden qualities."

"Hush your mouth. I don't want to hear that. You don't know Emma like I do."

"Is she a virgin?"

Alexis scowled a little harder. She shouldn't answer, but she was curious as to where Layton was going with his question. "No, of course not. She's not a nun."

"Then you have no idea who she is behind closed doors. Sometimes the most prudish people are wild things when no one is looking."

"Gahhh," she gargled, putting her fingers in her ears. "I don't want to speculate on my best friend's potentially freaky sex life—particularly when you're suggesting that she ought to hook up with my brother! *Ew.*"

Layton laughed, enjoying her discomfort. "You're adorably contradictory. One thing is for sure, one has to stay on their toes with you."

Alexis pursed her lips, unsure of whether she wanted to continue the argument or let it go, but Layton had already moved on.

"Well, there's nothing we could've done. Emma's phone died, which is why she wasn't answering, but they're okay and that's what matters."

"That explains it."

"Yeah…so they'll be back tomorrow after the car is repaired."

"What was he saying that made you look annoyed?"

He hesitated then answered, "Uh, he was telling me to keep my hands to myself."

"Too late."

"Yeah, that ship has sailed and it's not even circling the port."

She chuckled, but it brought up a bigger issue. "How'd he even know?"

"I don't know, big-brother sixth sense?"

"Maybe. Must've been in the tone of your voice or the inflection?"

"Who knows. But who cares? You're a big girl. You don't need your brother's approval for anything, much less who you date."

"I know, but like I said, the last thing I want to do is to come between you and Erik."

"It won't come to that."

Alexis nodded but her thoughts were wandering. The snow was still coming down in fat, lazy flakes, but the lights looked cheery and festive. Erik wouldn't admit it, but he liked when she decorated for the holidays. For Alexis, decorating for the holidays made them feel more real. She looked to Layton. "Want to help me drag the Christmas tree from the garage and start decorating?"

"Is there a second option?"

"Remember that thing I did right after the shower…"

He blushed a shade of red that didn't look natural on his skin tone, but she found his reaction cute. "Yeah," he choked out. "I remember."

"Well, I'll do it again if you help me get the tree ready."

He started walking briskly toward the garage. "Show me where the tree is stored. Let's get it started."

Alexis laughed and followed him out.

Two hours later, the tree was up and decorated and Alexis was beaming with excitement as the house started to look Christmassy. "Have I mentioned how much I adore Christmas?"

"You might've mentioned it."

"I do. I love it." She drew a deep breath and smiled. "'Tis the season to be jolly, you know."

But Layton only had eyes for her and even though she was delighted with the way the decorations had turned out, she couldn't ignore the pleasant tingle in her belly knowing that Layton was looking at her the way a wolf eyed a lamb.

The primal pulse of desire between them was almost palpable. So when Layton grabbed her and pulled her to him, she went with giddy anticipation.

He sank onto the sofa and she quickly straddled him. "This is going to be a hard habit to break," she told him between kisses. She reached down to fondle the bulge in his boxers. "How are we going to stop?"

Instead of answering, he pulled his erection free and she reached over to grab a condom from the box they'd left carelessly on the end table after their last session. Within seconds she had him sheathed and even faster than that, he was inside her. She shuddered as she came down on his cock, loving the way he stretched and filled her perfectly. She braced herself against the sofa cushions behind his head and slowly rode him, taking her time to savor each sensation as they built up the tempo and the rhythm. "Layton," she breathed, ending with a load moan. "Oh God, Layton…right there…"

He gripped her hips and helped guide her as he met her grind with slow thrusts and within moments, they were both nearing their edge. Layton reached down and pinched her throbbing clitoris, sending her hurtling into an epic orgasm that stole her breath and killed any semblance of lucid thought.

Layton tensed and shouted her name as he came,

thrusting hard into her sheath until he'd spent his load. She fell forward against his chest and for a long moment just focused on catching her breath.

Was it normal to be so consumed with another human being? Not even with Riker, who she'd been certain she was in love with, had she been so perfectly in sync. It was a little frightening, to be honest, that she was already questioning everything she thought she knew about herself. Was it possible to fall so hard, so fast for someone?

"Penny for your thoughts?" he asked in a husky tone that sent shivers down her spine.

She drew up, smiling as she traced her finger down his fine, muscled chest. "I was just thinking that I don't know what to do about you."

"What do you want to do?"

"Well, there is what I should do and what I want…"

"And?"

"And what I want is in direct opposition with what I should do."

"You're talking in circles."

"Yeah, welcome to my process."

Layton tightened his hold on her, anchoring his hands on her bare hips. "There are no guarantees in life, babe. We take our chances with what we've been given and you either have to have the balls to just go for it or live in the shadows of your life, always wondering what might've been. You don't seem to be the type of person who wants to live a half life. So grab life by the balls and squeeze."

"So you're saying I should just take a chance that you won't hurt me like Riker did and just let Erik know that we're testing the waters and then what?"

Layton caressed her cheek in a sweet gesture that plucked at her heart strings. "I'm not interested in a fling with you, Alexis. I'm not down with 'testing the waters.' I want the real deal."

She bit her lip. "What if I'm difficult and you discover that I'm truly a bad girlfriend? I get grumpy. And moody. And Erik says that I'm a slob. Can you deal with that?"

"Only one way to find out."

Was there nothing that she could say that would scare Layton away? "You're asking me to trust you."

"I am."

"I'm not really all that strong in that department right now." Her voice a tremulous betrayal of the anxiety twisting her nerves and making everything seem so dangerous to her heart.

He brushed a kiss across her lips. "Then let me help restore your faith."

And there it was. She had to take a leap to find out if there was firm footing when she landed. Riker had been a painful life lesson, one she was determined not to repeat, but as far as she could tell, Layton and Riker were nothing alike. So what was holding her back?

"I'm scared."

He gazed at her so tenderly that her heart nearly broke from the sweetness. Of course Layton was nothing like Riker. How could she even think that he was?

"We don't have to make big decisions right this second. Just give yourself permission to enjoy whatever this is…at whatever pace we deem appropriate but just know that I'm ready for the real deal with you."

"But what about Erik?" she asked, a little fearful of her brother's reaction. And what would her parents say? Ugh. She could already see her mother rolling her eyes at another one of her impetuous decisions.

"Erik isn't your warden," he said firmly. "Whatever is happening between us…it's private. No need for anyone else to weigh in with their opinions."

She liked Layton's no-wavering stance. He didn't back down at the hint of pressure. A man like that was handy to have around. A man like that was husband material— *Whoa, don't get ahead of yourself. There's no picking out the linens just yet.*

Layton tapped her behind and she lifted off him so he could discard the condom. She giggled at the most inappropriate thought. "We can never let Erik know that we've had sex all over his house. He will freak out. He's a bit of a germophobe."

"And he lets his messy sister live with him?"

Alexis shrugged a shoulder. "He loves me."

"Yes, he does. He's a good man, which is why I'm not worried. He might be pissed at first but he'll come around."

Alexis nodded, realizing that Layton was right. Erik wasn't an ogre and, generally speaking, he was pretty levelheaded. Not to mention, Erik had never truly been able to control anything Alexis did. Whatever Alexis put in her head she usually went after, no matter the consequences.

"I'm going to be unavailable a lot of times because of my school schedule," she warned, but she was already smiling because, oddly, it felt right. "I might be too tired for all this hanky-panky we've been doing all weekend. It won't always be like this."

"Thank God for that," he said. "I'm not sure I could live up to the hype," he teased and she laughed.

"You're a freaking stallion, who are you trying to fool?"

She snuggled up to him, loving how perfectly they fit together, whether they were banging the pictures off the walls or just watching movies. That felt like a sign—that the universe was trying to tell her something and she was trying like hell to listen this time around.

"I live at the station four days out of the week and I'm often on call, which means I could leave at a moment's notice, right in the middle of anything."

"I know. I'm used to it with Erik. Actually, I think that works out just right because I can't stand spending too much time with one person for an extended period. So, right about the time I'm starting to get sick of you will be the time you have to leave for your shift."

He laughed. "Sounds about right."

Wow. Were they really thinking of being together? She thought of Riker and how he'd burned her so badly, and now, everything she'd gone through with him seemed like a faint memory. There was one thing she had to say, though, before they embarked on anything resembling sharing a toothbrush holder.

Alexis rose up to meet Layton's gaze with all seriousness. "Do not abuse my trust. Whatever you do… just stay true. Can you do that?"

"I can do that," he agreed solemnly, sealing the promise with a kiss. "Now I just have one thing to ask, too."

She nodded. It was only fair. "Go ahead."

"I want to see you in a naughty-nurse costume at least once."

Alexis squealed and slapped him playfully. "Damn you, Layton, I was being serious."

"So was I," he quipped with a devilish grin, and she fell just a little harder for the man she never saw coming.

"Are you going to be a bad patient?" she asked coyly and he nodded vigorously. "Will I have to punish you?"

"Yes and yes."

She liked the idea of a power exchange. She'd never tried it, but damn if it didn't make her skin tingle at the fantasy.

"Are you game?" he asked, and she realized he was asking about more than just a kinky sex game—he was asking about it all.

Sobering, Alexis slowly nodded, her heartbeat fluttering at the implications of what felt like a momentous change in her life with that single affirmative nod.

Layton's arms tightened around her and she felt as if she'd come home after a long journey.

"Me, too," he said, sealing the deal.

And then just as he was about to kiss her, the lights dimmed and went out. She laughed. "Well, there goes the power. Now what?"

"Can't watch movies, can't bake…that leaves one thing," Layton said with mock resignation as he helped her from the sofa.

"Which is?" she asked playfully.

"This."

And then he shocked her by throwing her over his shoulder as if he was saving her from a burning building, and she squealed with laughter as he carried her straight to the bedroom.

He kicked the door shut with his foot and then gently tossed her to the bed and started to strip.

"Nothing to do but each other?" she supplied, enjoying the show as Layton got gloriously naked. Man, that body! She could swoon every time.

"You read my mind, babe." He grinned as he came toward her.

And then she was in Layton's arms, which, as it turned out, was the best place she'd ever been—or ever wanted to be.

The last thought zinging through her mind before she lost all sense of reasonable thought was...*Riker who*?

And that was the best feeling of all.

Layton was the best unexpected holiday gift of all time.

Merry Christmas to me! Fa-la-la-la-la, la-la-la-la!

Now, where to find a naughty-nurse costume... someone was going to get a spanking!

* * * * *

Dear Reader,

I'm going to confess that tossing a hot firefighter, a woman who's been crushing on him for years and a bottle of tequila into a cabin during a snowstorm is my personal catnip in a romance. Needless to say, writing Emma and Erik's adventure was a treat for me. In fact, the story flew out of my fingertips. And working with Kimberly Van Meter was the cherry on top of a pretty sweet book.

I hope you enjoy reading these fun stories of two best friends finding the perfect guys for them. And that they're both sexy firefighters? Well, that's *your* cherry on top.

Happy reading!

Liz

WHERE THERE'S SMOKE

Liz Talley

For Ike, Georgia and Deacon—my constant muses.
Thank you for the cold nose nudges,
the occasional doggy kisses and reminding me life
is fun.

1

ERIK MATHESON HAD fought a lot of fires, but he'd never been so damn tired before. Of course, a three-alarm blaze in an apartment complex was a rarity in the small town an hour north of Denver. And he was usually better rested before hitting his shift. Multiple late nights moving his sister back to Pine Ridge paired with accidental smoke inhalation had taken a toll. After knocking out the blaze, he could hardly stand on his own two feet.

"You okay, man?" Layton Davis asked, glancing over at him as they turned into the subdivision where Erik had bought a house a few months before. Layton shared a shift with him at the fire department.

"Yeah, I'm still kicking. But damn if I'm not beat."

"That's 'cause you're getting old," Layton said, ever the smart-ass.

"I've got five years on you. Not twenty." Erik rubbed his eyes. They still stung from the intense heat.

"Dude, I've never been to your place. Which way?" Layton asked, slowing the truck, his voice weary.

They'd been about to end their shift when the call came in. Being on their feet actively engaged in fighting the fully involved fire for over six hours had been brutal. Erik figured he'd sweated away the extra calories he'd packed on from all the Christmas cookies Alexis had been baking. His sister was a traditionalist when it came to the holidays, even forcing him to buy a Christmas tree and silly stockings to hang on his mantel. Since it was the first house he'd actually owned and his parents were currently in Scotland, he hadn't made too much of a fuss about his sister's attempt at an old-fashioned family Christmas.

"Take a left, then a right on Timber Ridge Drive."

Layton followed his directives. His younger friend was a solid guy, a little too pretty—a request from the Colorado firefighters' calendar project manager for Layton to model in the 2016 charity calendar had arrived last week. Poor dude had endured plenty of ribbing from the guys at the station. Good thing Alexis and her friend Emma were on their way to Colorado Springs and not still at his place. Alexis could never resist a pretty face, and she didn't need heartbreak on her menu.

"Right here," Erik said, pointing to the house with stacked stone columns and a wide front porch. His new place had plenty of room, which was a good thing, because the roads had already started icing up. No doubt his friend would have to stay the night.

"Nice place," Layton said, nosing the truck up the slippery driveway. The tires spun a bit, before catching and shooting them forward. "Damn, it's slick out."

"Which is why you're staying," Erik said, his words

sounding oddly slurred. Hell, he was more tired than he thought.

"Naw. I can make it back to my place. I'll swing by and get you tomorrow once the roads are clear and take you back to the station to get your truck."

"Dude, it's past one o'clock in the morning and the roads are shit. I have an extra bedroom."

"Thought your sister was staying with you for a while."

"She's in Colorado Springs spending the weekend with her best friend from high school." Her very grown and very hot best friend. Emma had stopped by yesterday as he was leaving for his shift. He hadn't seen her since she'd been in high school and he'd damn near choked on his hello. She was stunning, no longer leggy and awkward with braces. Emma Brent had grown into a full-fledged woman.

"I'll take you up on it. I could audition for the *Walking Dead*." Layton turned off the engine, glancing at Erik. "You need help?"

"It was a little smoke exhaustion. I'm fine." Erik opened the door and slid out, wincing at the sharp cold and the ache in his lungs. Toward the end of the fire, he'd slipped in the gook covering the ground floor when he entered a cleared room to set up the pressure fan. He'd knocked off his mask and couldn't get it back in place before inhaling too much smoke. He'd been cleared by the medics but had begrudgingly accepted Layton's offer to drive him home. Being light-headed and exhausted wasn't an appropriate mix for making it up the steep grade to his subdivision perched off Jackson Ridge.

By the time the men got to the porch, dodging the stinging sleet, Erik remembered he'd left his keys locked in the glove box of his truck. "Shit."

"What?" Layton asked.

"My keys."

Layton blinked in the glow of the porch light shaped like a lantern. "You're kiddin'."

"I have an extra. Wait here." Erik jogged around to the garage and lifted the speckled planter bearing the Christmas tree–looking bush his sister had brought him for a housewarming gift. The bottom bore a special compartment for a spare key.

Turning, he ducked his head down and ran back to the porch. "Got it."

A second later they pushed into the warmth of the house. Alexis had thoughtfully left on the light over the oven, casting a soft glow over the new furniture he'd picked out only weeks ago. The place still had new-car smell. Or rather, new-house smell.

"Let me grab you some stuff to change into. You'll probably want to take a shower." He glanced over at Layton, hoping his friend took the hint. Just about everything in the house was new, including the coverlet and sheets in the spare room his sister had been using.

"Thanks. Yeah, I do have to shower before I sleep."

"Me, too," Erik said, nodding toward the open door at the end of the hall. "Guest bath is through there. My sister's not exactly neat, but it should be clean."

"Don't care if it's not. I need a shower and ten hours of shut-eye. Just set the clothes outside the door. Night."

"Night," Erik echoed, trudging toward his bedroom with the en suite bathroom holding a steam shower. His room was dark and he didn't bother switching on the light. His eyes ached and his head throbbed. Smoke inhalation could make a person feel crappy.

Five minutes later he padded into his room, towel over his head. One more scrub at his damp hair and he tossed it in the direction of the chair that sat by his chest of drawers. He pulled back his covers and climbed into bed bare-assed naked, hungry for sleep and the warmth of his down comforter.

The first thing he noticed was how warm the bed was.

The second thing he noticed was the body curled up in the center of the bed.

The third thing he noticed was the scent of freshly laundered sheets.

And though his brain felt sluggish, he concluded pretty quickly that the person softly snoring in the center of his pillow-top mattress was his sister's oldest friend.

Emma Rose Brent.

His eyes adjusted to the moonlight streaming in between the curtains and he saw the outline of her body, the one he failed to see when he first entered his room. The light fell across her neck, highlighting her jawline and the loveliest pair of plump lips. For an upper-crust literature professor, Miss Emma Rose had lips that belonged in a porno.

And though his head pounded, his throat ached and his thoughts felt as jumbled as the storage room full of Alexis's junk, he couldn't help himself from drinking her in.

Emma had always been thin and awkward, stingy

with her shy grin. She rarely spoke, seemingly content to observe those around her, a shadow outside the spotlight. When he'd been around, she'd been especially quiet, so he'd been surprised at the confident woman who'd greeted him yesterday.

"Mmm," she murmured, turning over, pulling the covers with her.

This was so incredibly wrong, but he couldn't stop watching her. The wrinkle impression on her cheek, the tangle of her sandy hair, the small sigh of contentment escaping as she sank back into slumber.

And then his sister's scream shattered the silence.

EMMA HAD BEEN dreaming she was back in high school. Mrs. Vonnegut—not related to Kurt—had been fussing at her for screwing up the spring recital. She'd given Emma a piece she'd never seen before and instructed the orchestra to play along. Emma had struggled to keep up and Ertha Vonnegut had screamed at her to stop at once.

Then she woke up to someone actually screaming.

And noticed the man sitting next to her.

A naked man.

"Emma, Emma," the man whispered softly. "It's okay. It's me."

It took her a moment to register that the "me" was Alexis's older brother, Erik. "Wh-what are you doing?" she whispered as she scrambled away from him, clutching the covers in her fists, trying to figure out what was happening.

Erik was in bed with her. And he was naked. And Alexis was screaming.

"I'm sorry. I didn't know you were here," he said, grabbing the quilt at the foot of the bed and pulling it around himself.

"Alexis?" she whispered, still confused.

"Look, I'm sorry about all this, but I got to go save Layton. She's probably thrown something at him." Erik switched on the lamp, causing her to blink. The alarm clock on the nightstand showed her a steadfast 1:42 a.m.

Alexis had stopped screaming, but then a masculine yelp and curse followed.

"Too late," Erik said, rising, the patched quilt clutched around his waist. His broad back narrowed to a trim waist above the intriguing curve of his butt. She rubbed her eyes and zeroed in on his ass. Which she knew from past viewings was really nice.

There was a crash and then a wail.

"What the hell is going on?" she murmured as Erik opened his bedroom door. He'd taken only one step when another man, this one clad in jeans, came bounding by.

"Your sister's crazy, man," the guy said, raising his arms as if to fend off attack.

Alexis appeared, clad in a camisole and a pair of postage-stamp panties. "What the hell, Erik? Who *is* this?"

"Hey, hey." Erik caught his sister. Alexis looked ready to fight someone.

"Jesus, woman," the man beside Erik said. "I didn't know you were in there. Give me a freakin' break."

Emma remained rooted to the bed, covers tucked beneath her arms. She'd worn a T-shirt to bed, but her bra hung from the bedroom door and she'd shucked her pajama pants before climbing into Erik's bed. She tugged the covers up.

"What are you still doing here?" Erik said, gently pushing his sister back.

"Ow." Alexis winced as she stepped backward. She immediately lifted her foot and frowned down at the dangling appendage. "I think I hurt my ankle. And we're here because my memory sucks. I drove to pick up Em, but we decided to take her SUV from her place. Then just as we headed down I-25, I realized I left my laptop charger and we swung back because there wasn't going to be time to get a new one once we got to Emma's parents' place. By the time we could leave again, they had closed parts of the interstate. We figured we'd wait until midmorning to leave. Roads should be clear then."

"So that's why your car wasn't in the driveway," Erik said.

"Yeah. I thought you were working." Alexis hobbled into Erik's room and sat on the bed. Erik and the dude behind him watched as she tenderly prodded her ankle.

"Lex, you don't have any pants on," Emma whispered.

Her friend glanced up. "How different is this from my bathing suit? Crap, my ankle is really swelling."

Alexis was the person Emma wished she could be. Bold and confident, her best friend since third grade was a ball of energy, sass and smack talk. Being seen in her underwear didn't faze her.

"She punched me and then threw a shoe at me," the guy behind Erik said, sounding incredulous.

"You scared the crap out of me," Alexis retorted, her dark eyes blazing.

"Okay, okay." Erik held his hands up, pressing them against air. "Let's all just calm down. This was a big misunderstanding. No harm, no foul."

"Speak for yourself," Alexis muttered, her face twisted in pain. "I tripped over my suitcase when I was chasing that pervert out of my room."

"Pervert?" the guy said. "I'm not a—"

"He's not a pervert. Well, not usually. This is Layton Davis," Erik said, tilting his handsome face heavenward in what looked to be a prayer for patience. "He drove me home after we worked a blaze. I told him to take the spare room. I thought you were gone. You were supposed to be gone."

Guilt nudged Emma. Their being stranded was all her fault. She'd tried to run too many errands on her list that morning and it had pushed them back on getting everything done for the Christmas dinner and dance being held at the school her parents ran for mentally challenged adults. The party was scheduled for Saturday night and Alexis had volunteered to go with Emma to surprise her parents, who were receiving a community-service award at the annual function. Since Emma had recently moved to Greeley, which was just east of Pine Ridge, to teach at North Colorado State, she'd been thrilled when her bestie had suggested they make a girlfriends' weekend of it.

"Well, we weren't gone. And who doesn't check where he's going to sleep before plopping down on top of someone?" Alexis asked.

"Someone who's tired as shit and unaware someone's friend's sister is occupying the bed he was given," Layton said, flashing an annoyed glance toward Erik.

Erik shrugged. "Like I knew. Let's shelve the accusations and take a page from Emma's book and not freak out."

Everyone looked at Emma. She managed an awkward smile.

For a few seconds the room fell silent, the animosity dissipating.

"Okay, good. Now, since it's cold as frick outside and the roads are too dangerous, let's bunk up and get through the night," Erik said.

"Your sister probably needs an ice pack or something," Layton said, gesturing to Alexis, whose ankle looked swollen. "How about I grab some ice while you figure out the sleeping arrangements."

Layton disappeared and a light came on, lending a glow to the hallway.

"Why are you wearing a quilt?" Alexis asked.

"'Cause I'm naked under here," he said, tugging the quilt up higher. Emma had noted it slipped a bit during the whole Alexis-trying-to-kill-Layton incident, revealing washboard abs and the hint of the delicious narrowing to… No, she wasn't going to think about the crush she'd always had on him.

This was Alexis's brother.

And, yeah, he was hot as butter on a biscuit, but he was practically *family*. Erik was the guy who had given her noogies, who had pulled her pigtails. Okay, not literally, but pretty much the same thing. She wasn't supposed to notice the quilt dipping low to reveal the curve of his ass or how nice his naked torso looked or the fact he had a tattoo of an eagle on one side of his chest, which looked so…tough and male and—

"Wait, did you climb into bed with Emma while you were naked?" Alexis asked, still cradling her swelling ankle.

"Yeah," Erik admitted, looking unabashed.

Alexis glanced at Emma, eyebrows arched above amused eyes. "Well, how come you didn't scream?"

"I never scream." Emma sniffed.

"Well, if a big bozo sat on you, you would," Alexis grumbled.

The big bozo appeared with a bag of frozen broccoli wrapped in a dish towel. He frowned at Alexis but shouldered his way inside, handing the bag to her friend. "Here. I'm happy to take the couch."

"And I'll give you your bed back and sleep with Alexis," Emma said to Erik. "I feel so bad about being here when you—"

"I told you to," Alexis interrupted. "He was at work."

Erik looked as though he wanted to say something more, but he bit his tongue.

They all stood around. Finally, Emma said, "I'm not exactly dressed. And neither is Erik. So…"

"Right," Alexis said, sliding off the bed and hobbling toward the door. Erik frowned as if he wanted to help her, but he still clasped the quilt around his waist.

"Well, hell," Layton said, sweeping Alexis into his arms.

"Hey! Put me down," Alexis said, her nearly naked bottom staring Emma in the face.

"I will. In your room." Layton strode to the door, ignoring her friend's struggles. The man looked like a model, with hair flapping over one eye and sleek, knot-ted muscles bulging at Alexis's weight. Emma dropped her eyes down to Layton's tight butt and that's when she noticed Erik watching her.

She jerked her gaze away, begging the pink not to creep into her cheeks.

Which was a fail.

"Uh, I'm gonna grab some pants and then let you get dressed," Erik said, lifting her lacy pink bra off the doorknob. He eyed the sexy lingerie and then smiled as he handed it to her.

Desire punched her in the stomach.

Damn. Erik Matheson was an absolute fox. Layton may look like an Abercrombie model, but this man was like sex on a plate…just waiting for someone to take a satisfying bite.

Emma licked her lips before plucking the bra from his fingers. "Thank you."

"Need any help?" he asked, sounding serious, as his gaze dropped to her breasts covered by his blankets.

"Uh, no," she managed to say, her cheeks still likely bright red. Why couldn't she be like Alexis? Have the flippant, flirty comebacks? Be cool?

"I'm just kidding, Em," Erik said, grabbing his jeans off the chair in the corner and following Layton and his still-struggling sister from the room. Just as he was about to close the door, he popped his head back in. "Not that I wouldn't like to."

Then he shut the door, leaving Emma red-faced… but slightly turned on.

2

ERIK EYED THE ROADWAY, looking for patches of ice, and then glanced over at his sister's best friend. "The road looks okay. They're clear around Denver, but my buddy at highway patrol said traffic was still a nightmare. This shortcut will get you there faster."

"Good," Emma said, her hands folded primly in her lap. She wore a thick sweater with a scarf, a pair of black leggings and suede boots that stretched up her long legs to the bottom of her thighs. She looked amazing, especially with her blond waves falling over her shoulders and those pretty green eyes flocked by thick sooty lashes.

How in the hell would all those frat boys stay focused on Chaucer instead of their English lit professor's nice ass?

Probably with her cool demeanor. There was something so untouchable about Emma.

He'd insisted on driving her after fighting with a hobbling sister who had finally admitted she was in no shape to travel with her friend. Luckily, he'd showed no effects from the temporary smoke exhaustion. Apparently, eight uninterrupted hours of sleep worked wonders.

"Thank you again for driving me. I really wanted to be there to see my parents receive their award." Emma twisted her fingers and glanced over at him with those guileless green eyes.

"I wasn't letting you go alone in this weather, and, hey, at least I don't have to listen to Alexis bitch all weekend about her ankle."

"Poor Lex. Her ankle was so swollen. I feel bad for leaving her."

"It's a sprain. Layton said he'd drive her to get an X-ray, but it's not serious." Erik narrowed his eyes, looking for the turnoff. Normally, he'd never take a back road when the interstate and other well-traveled highways would be salted and much safer, but the dinner and dance honoring Emma's parents started in less than two hours. If Emma wanted to make it, then he had to make up for lost time. The ice storm had been bad and the interstate had opened a mere hour ago. Finding the correct turn, he slowed and carefully steered Emma's Lexus SUV onto the narrow two-lane highway.

Emma made a face. "I've never been this way before."

"I came this way all the time when I was in college. Don't worry. I've driven it in weather worse than this."

"I forgot you went to the Air Force Academy."

"For a year." He gave a shrug, slightly embarrassed he'd abandoned academia for something so mundane as being a firefighter. Deal was, he loved his job and knew it was where he belonged. Every hour he'd spent in a classroom had been excruciating. College hadn't been his cup of tea.

A few miles down the road that no longer felt familiar, he noted more frequent patches of ice. The road had been plowed at some point, but the salting had either been overlooked or the county hadn't bothered spending the money on a seldom-used byway. He needed to be very careful, so he decreased his speed and vowed to stop eyeing Emma's firm thighs. However, he could do nothing about the sensuous perfume that took his thoughts to places they had no business going.

The tires on the car slipped a few times, making Emma clutch the dashboard. "I'm sorry I'm being a nervous Nellie," she said, laughing at herself.

"Well, it's a bit worse than I remembered," Erik admitted, though he didn't want to state he'd been wrong about taking the shortcut. He probably should have stuck to the cleared interstate, getting Emma to the community center late, rather than trying to play macho hero. He'd just seen that look of longing in her eyes and wanted to impress her for some odd reason.

A sharp curve lay ahead and Erik tapped the brakes to slow down. Just as he started the turn, he hit black ice. The car slid sideways, veering toward the guardrail and a steep embankment.

"Ah," Emma squeaked as the back of the SUV fishtailed. He felt her grab the handle above her head but kept his eyes focused on the road and hands on the wheel. He managed to get control of the vehicle and had just breathed a sigh of relief when the back fender clipped the guardrail.

The Lexus did a 180-degree spin. The tires could find no traction as the SUV tilted backward over the embankment.

The seat belt jerked him against the seat and he heard Emma screaming.

Oh, shit.

He pressed the brake, locking up the tires, but he couldn't slow the momentum. They went down the steep embankment. Branches whooshed by and then the vehicle hit something that spun them another 180 degrees so that they were hurtling right toward a—

Huge tree.

The Lexus plowed into a bank of snow and then smacked the tree.

Hard.

His head snapped forward on impact and then something slammed into his body.

Air bag.

The entire time Emma had been screaming. Or maybe it was him? He didn't know. He couldn't see anything. He couldn't breathe.

Instinctively he fought the air bag, gasping for breath. The air bag immediately started deflating. "Emma?"

He didn't hear anything.

"Emma! Are you okay?" he shouted.

He heard the sound of spitting and then her hand connected with his leg. "I'm here. I think I'm okay."

Erik pressed down the expended air bag and looked over to find Emma covered in a powdery dust. Right when their gazes made contact, something slammed into the roof. She screeched, ducking down. He recoiled, too, before realizing the tremendous thump had been snow dislodging from the branches above them.

His heart beat in his ears and his body felt numb.

"Are you hurt?" he panted, adrenaline igniting, coursing through his body.

"I don't think so." She moved her legs, wincing a little. "My neck hurts a little, but I'm okay. You?"

"Yeah," he said, flexing his arms, wiggling his legs.

They'd been *very* lucky. The thick snow at the bottom of the hill had helped slow them before impact. If they hadn't had that bank of snow, they might have been gravely hurt. As a firefighter he'd seen plenty of head-on collisions.

The engine had died and he couldn't see anything through the spiderwebbed windshield. A fir-tree branch pressed against his driver's-side window, blocking his vision, so he looked past Emma, who still struggled with the air bag, to see they'd landed in brushy woods.

Erik breathed a sigh of relief when he pushed the unlock button and the doors made a telltale clicking sound. Then he unbuckled himself and dug his cell phone out of his pocket. He pressed the home-screen button and his apps appeared along with the signal display that read No Service. "Goddamn it."

He smacked the steering wheel, sending up a cloud of white powder that made him cough.

"What?" Emma said, stamping down on the fabric of the air bag.

"No frickin' service." He wagged his phone. "Try yours."

Emma unbuckled and felt around for her purse. Things must have fallen out, because she mumbled something that could have been a really naughty word before pulling out a pink phone with a bow on the top.

"Oh no," she breathed.

"What?"

"I forgot to charge it last night. Only one percent battery life."

"Who forgets to charge a phone?" he asked, feeling aggravation welling in him. It was like dealing with Alexis. No common sense. And now they had no way to phone for help.

Emma's eyes flashed fire. "Someone who was unfamiliar with the place she slept. Someone who had a naked man slide into bed with her. Someone who doesn't have to answer to you."

Touché.

Erik sighed and ran a hand over his face. "I'm sorry. Stress. Can't you charge it with the car battery?"

She ignored his apology. "Mine only charges when the engine is cranked. So who should I call?"

"That doesn't make any sense. It runs off the battery. Did you check your fuses?" Emma gave him a flat look, so he said, "Dial 911."

After getting the particulars about where he thought they were, Emma dialed the number. He watched, fear seeping into his gut. The temperatures weren't arctic, but they would drop when the sun went down. They needed to find help before that happened. He glanced at his watch: 4:33 p.m.

"Um, hi. Uh, my name is Emma Brent and my friend and I were traveling out here on—what's it called again?" She looked at him.

"Old Fox Farm Road," he said.

"You heard him? And we were cutting over to 105 when we hit some ice and ended up going over the shoulder, um, about ten miles past Mill Creek Run. Hello? Can you hear me? Hello?" Emma pulled the phone from her ear and looked at it. "No, no, no."

Then she lifted those pretty green eyes to him. "Sorry."

Erik wanted to slam his hand against the wheel again, but he didn't. "Okay. No big deal. I'm going to climb out and walk up the incline. I should have service once I'm on the road. You stay here. Put your coat on and stay warm."

Erik pulled his coat off the back floorboard and struggled into it. Tucking his scarf under the zipper, he opened the door, pushing hard against the bent metal, and climbed out into the bitter-cold day. Just as he slammed the door shut, sleet started falling, pinging on the smashed hood of the car. Not bothering to look over the wreckage, he began the climb up the steep embankment, praying that another vehicle might pass by, hoping beyond all hope he might get a signal.

Ten minutes later he turned and headed back down to the wrecked car. He'd not seen a single car pass by and his phone couldn't catch a signal no matter where he stood along the road. Which was ridiculous because every cellular commercial promised nationwide service. Such bullshit.

He pulled the door open to find Emma sitting bundled in her coat, teeth chattering. "Any luck?"

"No." He didn't want to admit how badly he'd fucked up by trying to take that shortcut. He'd gotten impatient about her phone not being charged, but the blame for this fiasco lay squarely on his shoulders. The only good news was that the sleet had stopped. But low mean clouds gathered in the distance. "Let's try to start the engine and charge your phone. Should have thought of that in the first place."

He pressed the button that should start the car. Nothing but a click. He pumped the gas pedal as if that would help. Nothing.

Emma pulled her hands from her pockets, holding her phone. "While you were gone, I managed to get my phone on again and sent a message to Alexis. I think it sent. Just said we'd wrecked off Old Fox and we were okay. That was the best I could do before it shut down again. I'm sorry I didn't charge it. We wouldn't be in this situation if I had."

Guilt sucker punched him. "No. This is my fault. I stubbornly insisted on taking this way."

"What are we going to do?"

"We're going to walk back to the highway and wait on someone to pass. It's a back road, but people live out here. Someone will come by."

No one came by.

It was like a movie. Two people stranded. Brutally cold weather. No one for miles. All they needed was an escaped serial killer.

"I can't believe this shit," Erik said, holding his phone up as they trudged back down the road in the direction from which they'd come. They'd waited for a car for a good thirty minutes before they decided to start walking. They'd only driven ten or twelve miles since they'd turned off the marked road. And the walking kept them somewhat warm. At least Emma's teeth had stopped chattering.

"Look," she said.

Erik had been moving his phone up and down, left and right, watching the left corner of his phone's screen. If he could just get one freaking bar. For the love of Pete, one bar.

Ripping his attention away, he followed her pointed finger to a small reflector buried in the grass.

Erik shoved his useless cell phone into his coat pocket and jogged over to the reflective glass. "I'll be damned. It's an old driveway."

3

EMMA WAS OFFICIALLY creeped out. The musty cabin hadn't likely hosted occupants in years. "This is so strange. Feels like a B movie and any minute a guy with a chain saw will pop out at us." She ran her gloved finger over the layer of dust on the small table.

"Already had that thought," Erik said, pushing the door he'd kicked in closed. The gray skies looked threatening and she could smell the snow in the air. Temps had already dropped since they'd hiked to the cabin.

The place was rustic...if run-down was considered rustic. But at one point it must have been a nice getaway. A small frozen pond sat just beyond, at the edge of the thick woods. The cabin was a one-roomer with a small kitchenette, a fridge and an unmade double bed. Faded gingham curtains hung in the two small windows and the decor was decidedly eighties with a focus on fish.

Emma pulled open the fridge and then immediately

closed it. It had been empty but smelled like death. "Ugh."

Erik rifled through a few cabinets. "Here's a flashlight that, uh, doesn't work. And a box of crackers dated 2001 and a tin of Spam. Matches." He shook the box.

Emma opened the only other door in the cabin and found a small bathroom with a toilet, sink and tiny shower. She twisted the faucet and water came out. "We have water," she shouted back to Erik.

"And the stove is gas. Though it's probably not hooked up any longer," Erik said.

"At least there's a fireplace." She pointed toward the empty grate. She walked over to the wood box. "Oh, and they left wood in the bin."

"I'll check the flue and then start the fire," he said, walking toward the fireplace.

"Does that mean we're staying here tonight?" she asked, knowing the answer but dreading his confirmation. A storm gathered outside and they were ill prepared...and very much alone.

"We'll have to. It's getting dark and looks like snow is on the way. We'll stay here and then tomorrow morning we'll head back to the road and try our luck finding help. Now, let me get that fire going. I'm frozen."

Emma plucked the matches from his hand. "You walk back to the car and get my luggage while I start the fire. I have some cookies and a wrapped tin of chocolates. It won't be much to eat, but it will be better than old Spam."

Erik looked as if he would argue, but instead

shrugged. "Okay. Check the flue and stack the wood. We'll light it when I get back."

"I can manage lighting a fire, Erik."

He pressed his lips into a line. "Look, I'm a firefighter and that's a fireplace that hasn't been used in years. Just let me have control of this one thing. Please."

She started to argue because he treated her like the kid she used to be. The awkward twelve-year-old who wandered into a beehive on the campout she'd gone on with his family, the newly licensed driver who had to call him to bring the gas can, the graduating senior who'd accidentally started a fire in the Matheson side yard on the Fourth of July. But Emma wasn't that gauche girl any longer. She could build a freaking fire without burning the place down.

But something in his expression stopped her.

Here was a commanding man accustomed to being in control of all things. At that moment he had none.

"Yes, Firefighter Matheson," she said, saluting and trying out a smile. If she was going to be holed up with a bossy firefighter in the middle of a potential snowstorm while missing her parents' award presentation, she needed to find her sense of humor.

And some self-control.

One bed, a roaring fire and the sexy guy she'd always had the hots for felt like an assload of temptation.

He looked hard at her and for a moment she wondered if he could see her thoughts. Did he know she wanted him…that she'd always wanted him?

No. She was the master of hiding feelings. Besides, Erik had never seen her as anyone other than his younger sister's nerdy friend.

"Okay. Stay here. Be safe."

A blast of cold air roared in when he opened the door. "Be careful," she called as he walked back into the world of white. If he was going to give orders, so was she.

Thirty minutes later, Erik pushed back in. While he'd been gone, she'd scoured the cabin looking for supplies. There wasn't much left behind in the place, but she'd found pillows, sheets and a few wool blankets in the bathroom closet. She'd aired them out, snapping them over the two tweed chairs centered in front of the fireplace. She'd also found some old rags under the sink along with a near-empty bottle of cleaner and had wiped down the counters and tabletop. The place still felt grimy, but at least now spiderwebs and dust weren't adding to the ambience.

"Jesus, it's cold outside," Erik said, rolling in her suitcase and dumping her emergency car kit on the floor. Inside, she had a first-aid kit and a few other things like bottled water, an extra blanket and a pack of tampons.

"And snowing hard," Emma said, watching as he unwound his plaid wool scarf from his head and shrugged out of his jacket. Snow coated his dark hair and he brushed it off. He wore a navy cable-knit sweater underneath, worn jeans and work boots. He'd been better prepared than she had. Her poor suede boots were ruined and the leggings she wore a flimsy barrier against the cold.

"You cleaned up a bit," he said, his gaze sweeping the place. When he looked at the bed, something hot slithered into her belly. "Brr, let's get that fire lit."

Emma dragged her damp suitcase toward the table and wiped away the excess moisture, glad she'd gotten a hard-shell case. Hoisting it, she pulled out the box of homemade chocolate-chip cookies along with the cylinder containing the expensive bottle of wine she'd gotten for her epicurean father. A flat box of handmade chocolates for her aunt Della also joined the stack. And as a plus, she found two protein bars she'd tucked into the pocket lining the case. Not the best dinner, but it would do until they could get back to civilization tomorrow.

The crackle of the lit fire drew her attention and instantly made the space cozy and—she licked her lips—intimate.

"Ah," Erik said, stripping off his gloves and warming his hands in front of the blaze. "Good thing this wood is aged and dry. Instant warmth. Come on over and warm up."

Emma hesitated for a moment, trying to regain a calm, less amorous demeanor. So they were alone in a cabin in the middle of nowhere with a bottle of wine, chocolate and a double bed? Big deal. She could handle it. After all, she'd never allowed her attraction for him to show through.

She walked over and crouched beside him, sighing at the warmth. Exploring the cabin had kept her moving, but her fingers and feet were numb.

"Here," he said, grabbing the nearest chair and dragging it close to the dancing flames. "Sit."

Seconds later they each sat in matching chairs, thawing out.

"I can't believe we're stuck here," she mused aloud,

the warmth making her drowsy. She suppressed a yawn. "This is like a movie I once saw."

"*Misery*?" he joked.

Emma laughed. "Are you planning on incapacitating me and making me write you a romance story?"

He wiggled his eyebrows. "That could be fun. But I could think of better things to do."

"Well, I saw some puzzles in the back of the storage closet. We can do one of those," Emma said, nervous about the direction the conversation headed. She wasn't a dumb-dumb; she knew that as a firefighter, Erik would never sleep with an unattended fire, which meant at some point he'd have to extinguish the fire. The room would get cold. Really cold. And there was that one bed sitting there like an elephant in the room… just not as noisy. Pair that with the fact she could easily be persuaded to find an upside to sharing body warmth and Emma could be in trouble.

"Are you suggesting rather than tying you up, I should do a puzzle with you?" he teased, hopping up to grab a blanket and place his scarf and coat nearby so they could dry.

"Or I can write that bad romance book."

"Or you can write a really good one. I'll volunteer for market research."

"Are you flirting with me, Erik Matheson?"

He grinned and crickets started hopping around her belly. Dang, but his smile could seduce a vestal virgin. He looked awfully yummy wrapped in a worn army blanket, hair ruffled from his trek through the woods wearing the scarf. Normally Erik was a buttoned-up sort of guy, which she totally dug. Nothing like a hard jaw, no-nonsense demeanor and a clean-cut style, but seeing him a bit smudged around the edges was a different turn-on.

How would he be in bed?

Commanding? Or content to let her take the lead? She could probably find out.

"Of course not," he said, sobering a little. "You're like my sister."

He said it as though he was reminding himself, which lessened the dart of hurt. He was right. They had been like brother and sister. Still, they hadn't seen each other in years. Emma was a whole different person from the girl she'd been when she hung around the Matheson house, scarfing down ice cream and watching 'N Sync videos. She'd graduated with a BA from the University of Colorado, completed her MA in comparative literature and was presently enrolled in a doctoral program. Not to mention she'd lost her braces, flat chest and virginity along the way. She most definitely was *not* his sister.

"If that's the case, you're a shitty brother. I haven't seen you in…seven years?" she said, jerking her head toward the blankets piled on the table. "Hand me a blanket?"

He tossed it to her and she tucked it around herself, sighing at the warmth. "How about some wine? Think we can find a corkscrew around here?"

"You have wine?" Erik shifted his gaze over to her.

"My dad's Christmas gift, but it must be sacrificed. And I pulled out the cookies and handmade chocolate, too. We may not have much to eat, but what we do have is the good stuff. Give me a few more moments of warm up and I'll wipe off a plate from the cupboard and make us dinner." She chuckled at the thought.

"Nah, I'm thawed out enough to do the dirty deed," he said, struggling from the depth of the chair. Emma snuggled into the dusty tweed warmth, trying not to think about spiders and other creepy crawlies that might have done the same over the years. She heard drawers slamming and Erik shout "bingo," then she heard the clink of glass and the pop of the cork.

"Let it breathe," she said.

"You're much bossier than I remember. Is that what they taught you in college, Miss Fancy Pants?" Erik asked, his voice light. Similar to how he'd talked to her when she *was* sixteen. "Hope you don't mind drinking out of water glasses."

"Of course not. Do you need help?" she asked.

"Nope," he said, sliding by her, holding two tall glasses with sunflowers etched on the side. He handed her both glasses then turned and grabbed the cleaned plate he'd loaded with the chocolates and cookies. *"Bon appétit."*

"It's a travesty to drink this pinot noir in such ugly glasses," she said as she held up the offensive glasses to the firelight. The vintage was brilliant ruby in the glow. It smelled as advertised, with notes of cherry, anise and sandalwood.

"What do you mean? My maw maw has these glasses," Erik said, settling into his chair, tugging the blanket around his knees. He balanced the plate of cookies in his lap.

That made Emma laugh.

"You're so different now," he said. The teasing in his eyes had disappeared and he stared at her thoughtfully.

"How so?"

"I don't know. It's like you're Emma, but you're not. Just different."

"Did you expect me to stay the same? I was a teenager. You should know that when you feed and water them, they grow up to become adults," she joked, swiping a chocolate off the plate and biting into it. "Mmm, these are so good."

She felt him watching her and something zipped in the air. Like the crackling of static electricity. Or the prickling of hair at the nape of her neck. She chewed the decadent candy she'd bought at Belvedere's when she'd gone shopping in Denver.

Turning, she caught him watching her, hunger present in his eyes. He blinked, cleared his throat and said, "I'm going to grab one of those jigsaw puzzles."

ERIK WAS IN TROUBLE. Not because he was stranded in a cabin in the middle of nowhere with no electricity and no way to communicate with the outside world. No. The danger wore diamond earrings and fuzzy wool socks. And she smelled like exotic perfume and had hair soft as spun silk. Not that he even knew what spun silk was. But it was probably soft since everyone compared soft stuff to it. Everything about her was womanly. She had curves that begged to be traced, plump flesh ready to yield to the hardness of a man.

Yeah, little Emma Rose was big-time trouble.

"You really want to do a puzzle?" she asked, her

tongue darting out to take care of the small chocolate fleck in the corner of her luscious lips.

No, I really want to do you.

But he couldn't actually say that to *her*.

"Uh, sure. We can drag the table in front of the fire. It would be easier to set the glasses and cookies on the table, too."

Emma made a face. "Okay, if you really want to." She struggled from the grasp of the scratchy blanket and padded in her socked feet to the small bathroom. A few minutes later she emerged with a water-stained box.

Erik jumped up and set about hauling the kitchen table as close to the fire as was safe. Then he moved the wingback chairs, already warm from their bodies, over to the table. He'd found a couple of candles on the back of a shelf in the kitchen, which he set on the table and lit.

The overall effect was very cozy.

Maybe too cozy for two single warm-blooded people drinking wine by candlelight.

"This was the best puzzle in the bunch." She held up the box showing a large whale breaching an Alaskan bay. Or somewhere cold. As if they needed something else to remind them of being cold and wet. Why couldn't the former owners of the cabin have bought a tropical-landscape puzzle?

"That'll work," he said, settling in the chair, pouring another slug of wine. Normally he went for beer, but he couldn't deny how warm the wine made him. "Let's try to create the border first."

Emma started flipping puzzle pieces. "I wonder if

Alexis got my message. I started to text my parents, but they'd have been too worried. They would have canceled the dinner. Ugh, it was so stupid to forget to charge my phone."

"You were out of your element," he said, finding two pieces that fit and tapping them down.

"I've been out of my element for a while now. Ever since I finished my master's, I've lived with my parents. It was easy. I taught high school, worked on my thesis and my mom cooked every night. It's not like I'm spoiled, but this past month of moving and starting a new job has been difficult. But I know I'm settling in to where I'm supposed to be."

"In academia?"

She nodded. "Hey, I've always been a nerd."

"Nothing nerdy about you, Emma. You're a beautiful, accomplished woman. I know your folks are proud."

Emma glanced up at him. "You're being awfully kind to the girl who broke your Stratocaster."

Laughing, Erik passed her a few pieces that looked as if they would fit the border she worked on. "I forgot about that. You should have stuck to air guitar."

"You were always nice to me."

He wanted to be nice to her now. Really nice. The fire cast a glow onto her golden hair, and her cheeks were flushed from the wine and heat. She'd abandoned her wool coat and the long sweater she wore molded to her high breasts. "Why wouldn't I be?"

"Some of my other friends' brothers were so nasty to their sisters. You and Alexis always had such a good relationship."

He shrugged. "My parents gave us no leeway for anything else."

For a few minutes they fell silent, sipping wine and squinting at the somewhat warped puzzle pieces. Every so often she shifted a certain way and he got a whiff of her perfume. Something about her sexy subtleness revved his blood.

He'd been single for half a year. His last girlfriend had been unwilling to move past anything casual. Not that Erik was jonesing to move toward the altar. He'd just wanted something more than casual sex and half-hearted dating.

"Are you seeing someone?" he asked.

Emma jerked her head up at his question. "As in dating?"

"Just wondering if you had someone significant."

She shook her head and something inside him did a tap dance. "I haven't had time to meet anyone since I moved to Greeley. I had been seeing a guy in Colorado Springs, but it wasn't serious. We agreed to end it when I made the move north."

"Oh."

"Why?"

"Just wondering. Casual conversation. Uh, so what are your plans for Christmas?"

"I was planning on staying with my parents until after Christmas then heading back to Greeley. I'm staying in a friend's duplex but need to find another place. He's in Italy and will return in the spring."

"It's just me and Alexis this Christmas. Mom and Dad went to Scotland for the holiday. That was their big dream—to visit my father's family."

"Good for them," Emma said, capturing her tongue between her teeth. She scrutinized the 982 remaining pieces. "I'm going to be honest, this makes me glad I have Netflix."

Erik chuckled, trying like hell to keep her from seeing just how much he was attracted to her. After all, she'd never given him cause to think she was interested in him in any other way than being Alexis's brother. "Yeah, peace and quiet sounds nice until there's no TV or Wi-Fi."

For the next few minutes while they completed the outline of the puzzle, they chatted about their favorite movies, TV series and the upcoming NFL playoffs. It amazed him that smarty-pants Emma loved the Broncos so much. All the while, he kept sneaking peeks at the way the firelight danced on her hair, at the way her plump lips teased him, at the way her breasts rose and fell when she laughed.

After an hour, they had a fourth of the puzzle completed.

"I need a break," Emma said, stretching her arms overhead and yawning.

"It's only seven thirty," he said after looking at his watch. Because that was safer than staring at the swell of her breasts jutting out as she arched back.

Damn.

He needed a cold shower.

Instead, he rose and walked over to the window, pulling back the dusty curtains. "Man, it's really coming down out there."

And then she was behind him, looking over his

shoulder. "Thank goodness we found this place. It might not be the Ritz, but at least we won't die."

"There's that," he said, turning back toward the room. She didn't move and only a foot stood between them. The air grew heavy with something he'd denied up one side of the room and down the other...but wasn't going away.

Emma raised her beautiful green eyes, her gaze meeting his.

For a moment he merely watched her. At the way her breathing increased, at those sweet, sweet lips. They were made for kissing and other things he couldn't allow himself to dwell on. When she licked them, it was nearly his undoing.

Almost family be damned.

A faint pinking of her cheeks gave her away. She stepped back. "Want another cookie?"

Inhaling quickly, he stepped around her. "Sure. I always liked dessert before dinner. Um, except I guess we're not having dinner."

4

WANT ANOTHER COOKIE?

Jesus, who said something like that to keep a guy from kissing her?

Because, if Emma were a betting woman, she'd lay a cool hundred down that Erik had almost kissed her.

And she'd allowed her cold feet to ruin it.

Not her literal cold feet, which weren't too bad now that the fire had warmed the room. But the cold feet sticking out from behind the flimsy curtain of propriety she'd strung across to hide her desire for the man she'd always wanted to take a bite of.

And why not?

What was the issue with having a fun little one-night stand?

After all, they were adults. Healthy, somewhat-horny adults with desires, needs and nothing to do but put together an old warped puzzle of a sperm whale. Not to mention Alexis never had to find out that she and Erik had entertained themselves by giving the old iron bed some action.

What Alexis didn't know wouldn't hurt her.

"You want a cookie, too?" Erik asked, jarring her from her internal argument over should she seduce him or shouldn't she. He wagged a cookie at her.

"No, thanks."

He took a bite and chewed thoughtfully. "You know, with the snow coming down as hard as it is, we might be stranded for longer than one night."

The desire she'd been flirting with took a backseat at the thought of them being in danger. They didn't have anything more than half a bottle of wine, a dozen cookies and two protein bars. "And my parents won't be worried because they didn't know I was coming. If Alexis thinks I'm home safely and my parents don't know I'm missing, the only shot we have is someone will miss you."

"But not until tomorrow. Alexis will assume I stayed the night because of the storm."

"Well, we can hope that the storm will be over tomorrow and we can head back to the road to look for help. Someone will be along at some point."

"Right," he said, grabbing another log and placing it carefully onto the blaze. The fire had warmed the room nicely, but because the wood was so dry, it burned fast. "Last one for tonight. We can't go to sleep with the fire roaring."

Unwittingly, she darted a glance to the bed she'd put sheets on. How in the hell were they going to make it through the night without things getting awkward?

He followed her gaze. "Don't worry. I can sleep here in the chair."

"But you'll freeze," she said.

"Let's not worry about that now. Want to work some more on the puzzle?" he asked.

She shook her head. "My eyes hurt from staring at the pieces in the low light." She walked back to the table and picked up the wine bottle and poured herself another glass. Then she sank back into the chair, tucking the blanket around her. "Tell me about being a firefighter."

"What's there to say? It's a job."

Emma tilted her head. "Not to you."

Erik's lips twitched. "Yeah, I love what I do. Nothing's better than pitting yourself against nature and winning."

"Never thought about it like that. Must be a high."

"To an extent, but there are plenty of boring days when we sit around the firehouse with nothing to do. It's feast or famine for an adrenaline junkie like me." He popped up, eyeing the trunk serving as a bedside table for a useless lamp.

"What?"

"Did you check that trunk?"

Emma shook her head. "Guess I didn't think about it."

Erik rose and walked over, setting the old lamp on the floor. One good kick to the flimsy lock and he had it unlatched. He opened the lid.

"Score," he said, lifting up a bottle of golden amber. "Tequila."

Emma hopped up and padded over to the treasure trove Erik had unearthed.

"Here's a pack of playing cards and poker chips. And—" he lifted up a box "—some condoms."

Emma took them from his hand. "So tequila and condoms. What did the former owners use this place for anyway?"

Erik lifted out a stack of magazines. They were an assortment of *Penthouse*, *Juggs* and *Hustler*. "I'm thinking whoever they are, they had some teenage sons."

"Well, thank goodness," Emma said, taking the tequila and the pack of cards. "We have a drinking alternative."

"What? You don't want the 1999 July issue of *Juggs*, too?" Erik cracked, dumping the magazines back in the trunk. "There's also some chewing tobacco, a pack of smokes and a box of peanut butter crackers. They expired in 2006 but I'm seriously thinking about eating some."

"They'd go great with the wine," Emma joked, setting the half bottle of tequila on the table along with the playing cards. "Or tequila."

Erik joined her, eyeing the barely put-together puzzle. "You want to adios Moby Dick?"

"If we do, we can play cards."

"Strip poker?" Erik asked, his eyes glinting naughtily.

This was her chance to flirt back, to let him know she wasn't opposed to dropping her clothes and making the best of a bad situation.

But did she want to go there with him? Sure, she'd wanted him only forever and a day, but if they got nasty, there was no undoing it. They'd have that between them forever. And that might get rough since both Emma and Alexis had moved within thirty miles of each other. More than likely she'd not go another seven years without seeing Erik.

"Well, if I had known we were going to play that, I wouldn't have drunk so much wine. I need my wits about me or I'll end up as naked as the day I was born."

"More wine?" he asked.

"You're a naughty man, aren't you?" she teased.

"You say that like it's a bad thing." Erik opened the warped puzzle box and slid the pieces inside, clearing the table. Then he removed the cards from the box and started shuffling them expertly. "And I will give you this one warning. While you're talking about Milton and Chaucer, I'm playing Mexican Sweat with the fellows at the firehouse. So if we go the strip route, you will be naked."

His blue eyes sparkled and he looked even more insanely attractive than normal. He'd skipped shaving that morning and now his face looked gruff and sexy. "You know I can't resist a challenge."

"My gain then because I'm betting you look spectacular naked."

Emma smiled. "Maybe you'll get to find out." She opened the tequila, not because she needed liquid courage at the moment. Okay, maybe she did a little. She wasn't like his sister who bought men drinks when they were at bars and dressed in tight dresses that showed off her curves. Emma had always been the more cautious of the two friends, but one thing she knew, she could hang with any man in the bedroom. "Now, what are we playing?"

Erik rattled off some game she'd never played, going

over the rules. Then they played a practice hand that he easily won.

"Give me another practice round…and another shot. Then we play for real." Emma said, feeling the warmth of the Jose Cuervo all the way down to her toes. Her tongue felt a bit thicker, her thighs tingly.

"You sure you want to do this?" he asked.

Something told her this wasn't just about the game. He knew what tequila, strip poker and a box of condoms could get them. He was giving her a way out, as only a guy like Erik could do.

Emma shrugged. "It's nearly a blizzard out there and we have to stay warm someway."

"That's usually not by taking your clothes off."

"Who said I'm taking my clothes off anyway," Emma said, giving him her best card-shark grin. "Deal me in, fireman."

AN HOUR LATER, Erik was down to his Calvin Kleins.

Emma, however, had only lost her pants. Even the fluffy wool socks stayed on her feet. And damn if she didn't look sexy in that sweater and fluffy socks.

"How did this happen?" he asked, truly baffled. He was good at poker. Really good. "You must be the luckiest woman I've ever met."

"Or really good at five-card draw," she said as she shuffled the cards and eyed his naked chest. "And from where I'm sitting, the view is very nice."

"Oh, now the cardsharp gets flirty," he said, lifting the tequila and taking a swig.

"Hey, I sang a burlesque tune when you took off your pants," she said.

And she had. Her green eyes had sparkled like emeralds in the light of the fire as she *ba-ba-ba-da-dummed* him as he unbuttoned his Levi's and shimmied out of them.

"I want you to know my feet are freezing," he said.

"Just one more hand," she teased, wiggling her eyebrows.

He nodded, hoping like hell he could keep his boxers on. Already he'd had an embarrassing thickening of his cock when she tugged off her leggings and again when she'd licked her lips. He felt like one of the boys who'd no doubt flipped through those girlie magazines. Horny as hell for Miss Emma Rose.

He dealt the hand. Emma rearranged the cards in her hand several times, frowning and making a moue with her pretty lips. "Hmm, I'm going to give these two and get two more."

He slid two cards from the deck and handed them to Emma then discarded three from his hand and took three new cards for himself.

He looked at his hand and nearly shouted hallelujah. A flush. "You in or out?"

Emma took five poker chips from the stack in front of her. "In."

Was she bluffing? No way could she beat him this time. That sweater was coming off. Or the socks. Please let it be the sweater. Please.

"You?" she asked.

He picked up ten chips, one that had the eye of the whale. "I'm in."

"Show me what you got," Emma said.

Erik laid down his cards, spreading them with flourish. "Boo-yah!"

"Oh, wow, that's really good," she said, her eyes widening.

"Yeah, so don't cry when you take off that pretty little top of yours."

Emma spread her cards. "But I think I'll keep it on." She had a fucking straight flush.

"No," he said, shaking his head. "No freaking way."

Emma grinned. "Hey, you dealt me those cards, and now I will take my prize. Off with the boxers."

Erik stood. "Are you cheating?"

"Absolutely not. I'm lucky, I suppose, so give me my prize, big boy," Emma said, clapping her hands like an empress.

He had to wonder if this was really Emma or Jose Cuervo talking because she was so, so, so different from the put-together, reserved woman he'd observed the day before. It wasn't that she came across as the shy-virgin type…just not a woman who would clap her hands and order him to remove his drawers.

"Are you sure?" he said, hooking his thumbs into the waistband of his boxers.

Emma only hesitated slightly before nodding. "Yeah, I want those cute little hearts to hit the floor."

Yeah, he had on the heart boxers his ex-girlfriend had given him a few years back. Not the most manly of underpants, but they were comfy.

"Okay," he said, jerking the waistband down.

Right at the moment he was about to clear his junk, the door to the cabin flew open.

Emma screeched as the door slammed into the wall,

making the cabin shudder. A gust of wind roared in extinguishing the candles and blowing the fire wildly, making embers and ash fly out of the grate.

"Shit," Erik yelled, not only because the wind was icy as shit, but also because embers from the fireplace scattered across the floor. "Get the door, Em!"

He lunged toward the fireplace, grabbing the puzzle box lid and slapping at the glowing embers that had scattered across the wooden floor.

"Holy crap," Emma said, pushing against the door, finally getting it closed. The busted lock had failed against the storm. Snow had spilled into the doorway. "I can't get it to stay."

Smacking the last of the burning embers, he stood and grabbed one of the kitchen chairs and wedged it underneath the doorknob, sealing the door and preventing it from blowing open again. "Thank goodness it opens inward. This should not only keep the storm from scaring the shit out of us again, but also slow down the chain-saw murderer who could show up while we're sleeping."

"Oh, thanks for making me feel safer," Emma joked, slumping against the door. "And now my poor wool socks are wet and I missed my reward for winning at poker. Did you plan that?"

Erik laughed. "Yeah, I have secret powers."

"Exactly what I was trying to find out with the removal of your undies." She sighed, a twinkle in her eyes.

"I can still shuck them," he said.

She shook her head, making her honey waves tumble seductively. Or maybe it just seemed seductive because neither one of them was wearing pants.

"Nothing like a windchill of five below and a pair of cold wet socks to sober a girl up. Keep your hearts on, big boy," she said, moving past him, snapping the band of his underwear.

And damn, if that wasn't the sexiest thing a woman had done to him in a long time.

So confident, so breezy…and it had nothing to do with the wind that had just blown through.

"You want to play some blackjack or something?" he asked, moving back to the table where Emma perched on the arm of the tweed chair, tugging off her socks. "Hey, if I knew that could get you out of your socks, I would have summoned the wind earlier."

She smiled and said, "So, do I get some burlesque music?"

"Only if you do it sexy," he joked as he tugged on his shirt and jeans. He found one of his socks on the back of the chair, the other near the fireplace.

"I'm not sure you can pull polka-dot fuzzy socks off in a sexy manner," she said.

"So blackjack?"

"Actually, I'm tired," she said, eyeing her suitcase. "I brought some flannel pajamas and extra socks. Just going to slip into the bathroom and put them on. And brush my teeth."

"Oh, sure." He didn't have anything to change into. Not even any deodorant to freshen up with or a toothbrush.

"Uh, I have an extra toothbrush you can use if you want. I always carry an extra in my toiletry bag. Unfortunately, I don't have anything for you to sleep in. Unless you like lacy lingerie."

"You have that with you?" he asked, his mind immediately flipping to the image of Emma in pink silk and lace. A most delicious fantasy.

"No. That was a joke, silly." Emma grabbed her suitcase and rolled it behind her to the tiny bathroom.

Erik dashed the kinky vision from his mind. He had to if he was going to survive the night with her without giving in to something that probably wasn't a good idea. After all, he couldn't seduce his sister's BFF, could he? Of course, after their game of strip poker, he wasn't so sure he'd be the one doing the seducing. Miss Emma Rose held her own. Still, where would they go from there? Emma wasn't the kind of girl a guy had a one-night stand with. Yet maybe it didn't have to be a one-night thing, maybe…

He looked up to find her staring at him with a quizzical expression. "Uh, you go ahead and get ready. I'll put another log on to give us some heat. That gust of wind made it too cold in here."

"Okay, thanks," she said, disappearing into the bathroom.

Closing his eyes, he sucked in a breath. He needed to get ahold of himself and remember they were in a dicey situation. Sure, things could be worse. They had found shelter from the storm and had some food…if cookies and chocolates counted. Not to mention a nice fire and a place to bed down. But still, if things deteriorated with the weather or if no one came to find them, they could be in trouble.

Before stoking the fire, he grabbed the large pot

he'd spied under the sink and wiped it out. Filling it with water, he took it to the hearth and set it as close as possible to the fire. It was too late to wash tonight, but some lukewarm water for a spit-shine bath might be good in the morning. By the time Emma emerged from the bathroom, he had the fire crackling once again.

"Feels much better in here," she said, lugging her suitcase behind her. She wore mint-green pajamas with puppy dogs frolicking on them. It was a firm reminder that this was the kid who'd hung out at his house wearing flannel shirts and ripped jeans, braces flashing when she gave a rare smile. Emma wasn't a sex kitten…even if she'd behaved like one.

"Nice puppies," he joked.

Her cheeks pinked. "Yeah, they're silly but warm."

"And new fluffy socks."

She lifted her foot and twisted it back and forth. "Only the latest in fuzzy haute couture."

She joked but she looked nervous. Like a patient awaiting the dentist. Something about it was endearing. "You know I'm not going to pounce on you."

Pressing a hand to her cheek, she said, "Oh, jeez. Give me some credit. I know you're not interested in me that way. I'm your sister's friend. You said yourself that I'm like family. It's just weird to think about sleeping with you."

"For one thing, we're *sleeping* together. Not having sex. Think of it as a survival thing and not a big deal." Much. He knew that it would be hard not to touch her when they climbed beneath the scratchy wool blankets, especially since they'd already been a little naughty by shooting tequila and playing strip poker. Who did that with someone he professed to be like his sister?

But she wasn't his sister, was she?

And she was no longer that little girl who stared at him with yearning eyes.

"But don't fool yourself into thinking that I don't think about how you'd have looked in your undies. You're a beautiful woman who is *not* my sister. I'm really pissed I dealt myself shitty cards."

The darkening of her pink cheeks had nothing to do with the warmer room. "Oh."

"So where's that extra toothbrush?" he asked.

5

EMMA SANK ONTO the bed while Erik took a turn in the bathroom.

Oh, come on, silly. It's no big deal. It's like sitting next to someone on the train. Except you're lying down. In your favorite dog pajamas.

Minutes before, she'd been warmed by tequila and wine, feeling a bit saucy and bold. That girl didn't care if Erik lay next to her. That girl wanted him next to her. So why was she having such misgivings?

Because a gust of wind cooled her ardor?

Or because she was truly afraid of herself?

That image of Erik standing before her, sliding his boxers down had imprinted in her mind. It was like a sexy GIF that kept repeating, revving her up. Making her want to see more. Do more with the guy she'd dreamed about her entire junior year of high school... all because of that one summer night.

She'd seen him in the Mathesons' pool with a girl.

Sleeping over at Alexis's was a weekly deal in the summer. Erik had dropped out of the Air Force Acad-

emy and was in the middle of firefighter training. He'd
moved back to his parents' house to save money, but
he was rarely around. But one weekend the Mathesons
had gone to Vegas, leaving Alexis at home with Erik.
He'd been sidelined. Rather than go out, he'd brought
home the fun. In the form of one Whitney Kellogg.
The beachy blonde had been the head cheerleader at
Pine Ridge Academy and made wearing short shorts
and knotted plaid shirts that showed her tight belly an
art form. With more curves than a mountain road, the
perky Whitney was the antithesis of Emma.

All weekend Whitney had perched on the arm of
Erik's chair, swigging beer and laughing with the most
annoying bray. She'd touched him all the time, too. But
then Saturday night, Emma had padded into the kitchen
to get some markers for the project she and Alexis were
working on and she'd seen them in the pool.

The moon had been full that night, framing the two
lovers in the water. Erik stood in the middle of the
pool, kissing Whitney and untying a string bikini that
looked like a rubber band trying to hold back toddlers
at a playground. The fact it hadn't already snapped
and rendered Erik unconscious was a miracle in itself.
But now he was intentionally taking it off. And Emma
couldn't look away.

It was like a car wreck—visceral, horrible and oddly
fascinating.

His lips had traveled down Whitney's jaw to her
neck, as his hand slid up to cup the gargantuan boob
that had escaped the constraints of the bikini.

And pervy Emma had stood there, watching, wondering what it felt like…to have his hands touch her there, to have his mouth slide down and—

She had turned away, knowing she couldn't continue to watch them do it in the pool.

But at the same time, she'd been so turned on. Not by vapid Whitney of the Big Boobs but by the sensuality of Erik. He hadn't been like dorky Tyler McMurty who'd tried to feel her up in the church van with not so much as a how-do-you-do. No, Erik knew what he was doing. He was like a guy in a movie, gorgeous, sexy and knowledgeable.

And so she'd become obsessed with him that summer. Every time he was around, she couldn't keep her eyes off him. Alexis noticed, of course. Her friend noticed everything. She was a regular ol' Nancy Drew type. And she'd said things like "Stop looking at him like that. It's so gross."

But nothing about Erik was gross.

Actually, quite the opposite.

Erik Matheson became her ideal.

Now, the door opened and Erik emerged, still wearing a sweater and jeans. Disappointment at not getting another glimpse of the flesh she'd seen earlier that night filled her.

"Whew, that water was cold as hell," he said.

"I know. My teeth felt frozen."

"I set a pot of water by the fire. Figure tomorrow morning we'd light the fire again and it would get lukewarm enough to wash up with."

"Good thinking." She wondered if she should get up from the bed or fake being super sleepy and say goodnight. Those infernal crickets that always showed up when Erik was around started chirping and hopping in her belly.

"I'm going to sit here for a few minutes and let the fire get low. Want to make sure we're safe tonight."

"Okay, I guess I'll go ahead and go to bed," she said, rising and picking up the blanket she'd left on the chair. Another one lay folded on the kitchen counter and Erik had already tucked the third one around himself. With three blankets atop the faded sheets, they should be warm enough. She set about placing the blankets on the bed and fluffing her pillow while Erik sat staring thoughtfully at the fire. Her actions were a bit sloppy because she still felt the effects of the booze she'd consumed. She wasn't drunk, but maybe a little tipsy. The snap of cold wind earlier couldn't erase two glasses of wine and a shot of tequila. Or was it two shots of tequila?

With nothing else productive left to do, she slid into the double-size bed. The sheets were like ice and so she swished her fuzzy-socked feet back and forth to warm the bed, drawing his attention.

"Cold?" he queried.

"Freezing."

"Go ahead and warm my side, too."

"Fat chance," she said, cracking a smile.

"I always wondered what you and my sister did during all those sleepovers. Should I expect to get my hair highlighted and have a spontaneous pillow fight?"

Emma punched the pillow and sank onto it, ignoring the musty smell from no doubt being stored for too many years. "Guys have weird fantasies about that, but to tell the truth, most of the time we watched a movie or worked on class projects."

"Ah, I forgot what little nerds you were," he teased.

"Little nerds grow up to be successful women, thank you very much," Emma said, lifting her nose in the air and giving a sniff.

"Indeed you did," he said. "I'll try not to wake you when I slip into bed. I know it feels weird, but you're right. If I tried to sleep in this chair, I'd freeze once the fire died. We're big people. We can handle this, right?"

Maybe. When said out loud it made a good deal of sense. Body heat and all that, but the reality of the situation was they'd been flirting with each other all night. And though she had worn her bra under her jammies and he would no doubt still be dressed in some manner, they would be more intimate than they'd ever been.

And with the torch she'd always carried for him re-ignited, it wouldn't take much before she'd lose all rational thought. She was primed to go up in smoke for this firefighter.

"We can handle this. Good night, Erik."

He smiled. "Good night, Em. I had a lot of fun to-night. Maybe I should get stuck in snowstorms more often with you."

Emma lay back, pulling the covers to her chin, bur-rowing as best she could into the lumpy mattress. A broken coil prodded her, so she curled on her side, scooting to the right, leaving Erik the left side. At some point they'd brush against each other. There would be no way to prevent it. Erik was a decent-size guy and she wasn't exactly petite.

She wouldn't be able to sleep.

No way she'd be able to with her stomach doing loop-de-loops and feet cold as Popsicles.

Sighing, she flipped over onto her belly, a tried-and-proven way to relax herself. With the fire crackling and the bed finally growing warm with her body heat, she found herself sliding from thoughts of her evening with Erik to regret about her poor car and missing her parents' award presentation. Nothing that couldn't be fixed or remedied by a YouTube video that her brother had promised to post, but still a loss. And then there was the fact the roads might be too bad tomorrow. Alexis might not have received her text. But she'd be worried about Erik. She'd call both of them and not get an answer. Her friend wasn't the kind of girl to sit on her laurels. No, Alexis would send out the cavalry. And someone would find them tomorrow.

And then a fox appeared, sniffing the snow, making little paw prints.

And then she drifted off.

ERIK WATCHED THE fire until only a small flame remained and then he pulled the dusty fire screen in front of the hearth, assured that no small sparks would escape and ignite on the scraped wooden floors. The room was plenty toasty and he had to send a silent thank-you to the man who had built a one-room cabin rather than a much larger place. Easy to heat.

Emma breathed rhythmically letting him know she was asleep.

Which was good.

That's why he'd stayed awake. Oh, sure, the fire and all, but he knew he couldn't lie there with her awake, knowing that he wanted to do more than sleep. Knowing that she probably wanted the same thing.

Deal was, nothing about it was a good idea. Except the pleasure it would bring. He had no doubt they'd be good together. Beneath Emma's cool intellect burned a passionate, funny woman. But they were from two different worlds. She with her highbrow professor friends and he with his lowbrow good ol' boys at the station. The only opera they would consider watching would be *Days of Our Lives*. And that was only because Grant Teague claimed he had to be able to talk about it with his mother who was in assisted care and obsessed with the show. Erik suspected Grant was addicted to the show and needed a reason to watch.

And then there was his sister. Alexis loved Emma. Even when Alexis had moved away, she planned girls' trips with Emma and he knew they spoke daily. If things went south between him and Emma because they gave in to desire, there would be hell to pay. He didn't want Emma hurt. Hell, *he* didn't want to hurt. But he damn sure didn't want his sister up his ass about being a hound dog and messing with her friend.

So, yeah, he let Emma go to bed and waited for her to fall asleep. Might have been cowardly, but he knew it would be an added protection against anything happening between them.

Slowly he rose and walked to the bed. Emma lay on her side, waiting like a gift beneath his Christmas tree. Tawny strands of gold spilled off the pillow she'd punched into a ball. She looked angelic.

Yet he still wanted to gather her to him and slowly unbutton her puppy-dog jammies.

Tugging off his jeans, he lay them on the ransacked trunk filled with girlie magazines. Then he shucked off his sweater, leaving him clad only in his boxers, undershirt and socks. Not the sexiest of outfits, but he'd be way more comfortable.

Carefully he pulled the blankets back and eased ever so gently into the bed. Luckily his side was warm because of Emma's body heat. It took a minute for him to fully relax, mostly because the pillow was total crap and the sheets smelled like his aunt Marmie's house.

But then he caught the scent of the warm woman sleeping next to him. She wore some sultry perfume that smelled like a field of flowers and money all rolled up into one. And she snored softly. Nothing obnoxious, just little puffs of air.

He carefully rolled onto his side, turning his back to her and tucking up the covers. The bed was a bit hard and sprongy, but he'd slept on worse. Closing his eyes, he vowed to fall asleep.

But then she turned over and snuggled up to him, her hand inching across his waist. And that was all it took for his cock to twitch.

Jeez, what the hell. He reacted like some knock-kneed schoolboy who'd never gotten laid before. But obviously that part below his belt hadn't gotten the memo that nothing was going to happen.

"Mmm," she moaned, snuggling into him, tucking her legs up so they fit the back of his thighs, her warm breath penetrating the cotton of his undershirt.

"Emma?" he whispered.

"Mmm?"

"Nothing," he said, because if he asked her why

she'd cuddled up next to him, she'd withdraw. And if he had to sleep with a hard dick, he'd do it. Because the feeling of her pressed next to him was worth the blue balls he'd wake up with in the morning.

He let loose a sigh and stared at the rough-hewn wall. The low light from the fireplace tossed shadows against the grain.

Emma's hand flattened against his belly, moving ever so slightly, almost a caress.

Pure torture.

Her breathing changed and it was at that moment he knew she'd woken.

"Emma?" he whispered again.

"What?" she whispered back.

"You can't keep doing that."

"Doing what?" she whispered, her hand stilling.

He turned over.

She didn't move, her hand fell across his abdomen and her head dropped just beneath his shoulder. Sleepy green eyes met his gaze. "What are you doing?"

"Trying to stay warm," she whispered.

"Oh," he said, wrapping an arm around her and pulling her to him. She lifted her head onto his shoulder and even her knee crooked over his leg slightly. He set his hand on her shoulder, rubbing it to warm her. She felt plenty warm, but the fire had nearly died out and the insulation in the small cabin didn't look up to date.

Raising her hand, she set it on his chest.

"Your heart is beating fast."

No shit.

He was a hair's breadth away from rolling her onto her back and showing her just how much he wanted her. With every fiber of his being he wanted to sink inside her and lose himself in something so good. It took every ounce of strength he had to reach up and grab her hand. "Em, you're playing with fire. I have pretty good self-control, but just so you know, I'm on the edge, sweetheart."

"What if I want to go over the edge with you?" she asked, lifting her head slightly and studying him.

He couldn't see if she was being a tease or serious.

"Have you thought about what that would mean?"

"Yes, but no one will ever have to know, would they?" she asked, wriggling her hand from his grasp. She petted his T-shirt seductively. "I mean, we don't have to tell. It could be like a little secret. Like one of those things that happen at a party when you're drunk...and you never talk about it again. Pretend it away."

Briefly he closed his eyes because he really wanted to do as she suggested. Opening them, he said, "Can you handle that?"

"Sure I can," she said, but her words seemed hollow. As though maybe she wasn't the kind who could ever handle a true one-night stand, no matter how much she wanted to believe it. But was that his problem?

"I don't think—"

"Maybe you shouldn't think," she said, pressing a finger against his lips. "Thing is, Erik, I'm a big girl now, a big girl who knows what she wants. So you either want me or you don't. And honestly, you not wanting me might be ten times worse than you and I having crazy cabin-fever sex."

"Not want you?" he asked, finding it incredible she didn't already know how hot for her he was. "Here."

He grabbed the finger that had slid down to imprint the cleft of his chin and tugged her hand downward to the raging erection he'd had since she'd first draped her hand over his waist. Placing her hand on the length of himself, nearly coming at the contact of her fingers, he said, "Does that feel like I don't want you?"

"No, it doesn't," she said, fitting him to her palm.

"Oh, uh," he groaned, wrenching her hand away before he made a total mess of the sheets. Again, he wondered how she'd relegated him to a green boy, inexperienced to such a degree he ejaculated on first contact. "I think we better slow down, Miss Emma Rose."

"So are you going to warm me up, Matheson?"

He laughed and lifted himself on one elbow, pushing her back onto the creaky bed. "Oh, I'm about to see what lies beneath those puppies."

Emma laughed and brushed her hands across his forehead, capturing a loose lock and twisting it around her finger. "I knew these pajamas would drive you mad. That's why I left my fancy lingerie in the suitcase. I could see right away you were a dog man."

Erik looked at her face in the dying embers of the fire. Conviction sat in those emerald depths, in the set of her chin. He'd never known she was so stubborn. This Emma was no delicate flower waiting to be tended. This Emma was a woman who asked for what she wanted.

What she wanted was him.

And that was damned sexy.

6

EMMA COULDN'T BELIEVE she'd made the first move.

She'd slept for a good fifteen or twenty minutes while Erik waited on the fire. But when he'd sneaked into bed, she'd felt him…this time. A night ago, at his house, she'd been so unaware and so tired from moving, she hadn't felt him climb into bed. But tonight, she had a hyperaware thing going on. She'd thought about it for a few minutes, faking sleep.

Her mind kept flipping back to all those times she'd clammed up when he was around, tongue-tied and gauche. A girl who didn't think she was worthy of a stud like Erik. So many opportunities to talk to him, to flirt even, washed away because she was too afraid to be vulnerable. Even last night, when he'd climbed into his bed naked, she'd acted shy. But she wasn't that woman anymore, damn it.

She'd grown, gained her wings and thanks to Alexis, she had started asserting herself.

Okay, this was truly the bravest she'd ever been.

But when she'd thought about going back to the real

world, without taking the opportunity to be with Erik, she felt disappointed in herself. She knew he wanted her. And she wanted him. So what was the big deal? Fear that their virtually nonexistent relationship might be damaged? Fear that Alexis might get miffed?

No.

None of that was reason enough to pass up what she'd always dreamed about.

Being Erik Matheson's girl…for at least one night.

So now she lay beneath him, looking up at the sexiest man she'd ever seen—she lifted her hand and caressed his cheek.

"You're so damn beautiful, Emma," he said.

She couldn't see his eyes, but she felt him take her in. Her pulse sped up and her breathing amped. "Kiss me. Please."

Erik lowered his head and nipped her lower lip with his teeth. It was erotic, making her nipples harden and liquid heat pool inside her. Then ever so softly he traced her bottom lip with his tongue. "Mmm, you taste good, Em."

"I brushed," she whispered.

A flash of white teeth and then he lowered his head again. This time he pressed his lips against hers, light as an angel's kiss.

She moaned and lifted her head.

"Oh no, sweet girl. I want to take my time with you. I want to tease you, drive you crazy, until you beg. Will you beg me, Emma?"

Emma nearly lost her breath. She'd imagined Erik as her lover many times before, but she'd never guessed he'd be so…erotic. He wanted her to beg.

Well, she wanted him to make her beg.

Dropping her head back, she said, "Let's see what you can do."

He started unbuttoning the top of her flannel pajamas. "First I want to see you. Then I'll kiss you."

A slave to the desire unfurling inside her, she could only nod and watch him as he slowly unbuttoned, pausing at every button to deliver a kiss on her flesh as he peeled back each layer.

"Oh, you wanted to make it harder for me," he said, fingering her nipple through the lace of her bra. Emma inhaled audibly. "That's okay, sweetheart. I love a challenge."

Then he bent and sucked her nipple into the wet heat of his mouth.

"Ah," Emma said, arching toward him.

The devil laughed, nipping her with his teeth before releasing the rosy nipple.

Once the pajama top lay open, he reached for the drawstring of her pants. Tugging them, he gave but one command. "Lift."

Emma did as she was bid, raising her hips so that he could pull the flannel pants from her body. Languidly he tossed them toward the foot of the bed. Running a hand down one leg and back up the other, he boldly traced a finger through the damp lace at the juncture of her legs. "Oh, good girl. You're already so wet. Do you know what that does to me? Oh, I think you do, baby."

She reached for him, drunk with passion. She needed to touch him. Use her mouth on him. Something. Anything.

"No, no. There will be time for that later. Right

now, I have a mission. You remember what that was?" he asked.

Emma nodded.

"What?"

"You're going to make me beg," she whispered.

"Mmm-hmm," he said, lifting himself up and settling his body onto hers. His erection pressed against her thigh, a portent of what would come.

Then he started kissing her jaw, nibbling a little path down her neck, across her collarbone and back up to her lips.

Emma panted, no other way to put it. Liquid heat soaked her, and her lower pelvis ached to be filled. She could feel how wet she was, soaking her panties with slickness, permeating the air with the smell of arousal. She opened her mouth to say "please," but then remembered. She wanted the torture Erik seemed intent on providing.

Finally, he caressed her jaw, tugging it lower, opening her mouth to him. Then he pressed his lips to her, tenderness gone, as he plundered her mouth. She met him eagerly, kissing him back, tangling her tongue wildly with his. Her heart galloped and she felt nearly frenzied. She'd never felt this way. Never so out of control.

Instinctively she raised her hips, opening her legs. Erik took the hint and slid so he fit between them. Then he rocked his hips, allowing the rigid length to slide against her slick heat, driving her crazy.

One hand twined in her hair as he continued the onslaught on her mouth, his tongue parrying against hers, leaving her nearly sobbing for release. She'd never felt so out of control, so caught up in desire. Finally, he lifted his head and made his way down to her neck. His beard prickled her skin and it should have irritated, but instead it was another sensation vaulting her toward what she craved.

With one flick of his hand, he released the front clasp of her bra and cupped her breast.

"Ah, so, so pretty, Emma. Like small rosebuds," he said, capturing one peak with his teeth, biting softly before sucking her into the heat of his mouth.

"Oh, oh, yes, pl—" Emma groaned.

He lifted his head and quirked an eyebrow. She bit down on her tongue, making him laugh. "Close. Very, very close."

And then he bent his head again, giving equal attention to the other breast. Emma squirmed against him, enjoying the feel of his hardness sliding against her sensitive flesh. He did amazing things with his mouth. She'd never been so stimulated by her breasts.

His hand traveled down to her hip, stroking, squeezing, pleasuring her. And then his mouth was on hers again, and she knew by the way he kissed her that his control was on a short leash.

Their breaths mingled, soft pants of urgency.

Erik slid down the length of her body, bestowing a kiss on each tip of her breast before using his scruffy beard to tantalize her belly. He dropped little kisses down to her navel before slithering so he knelt between her legs.

Rising, he pulled his T-shirt off, revealing a chiseled torso. He had a fine sprinkling of hair across his chest that converged into a darker Y between his pecs.

The screeching-eagle tattoo swooped down from the left side of his chest, lending a roguishness to him. His waist was trim and stomach tight enough to show the hint of a six-pack. Emma had never been with a man so manly. He was like a lumberjack or a Viking...or just a superhot firefighter.

Lifting herself on one elbow, she reached out and traced a finger down his stomach, enjoying the way his flesh contracted. She hooked a finger in his boxers, which were tented from the large erection straining against the cotton. "My turn?"

"No." He smiled, capturing her hand and bending to bestow an almost courtly kiss on her wrist. "You haven't begged yet. So—" he pushed her back onto the subpar pillow "—I need to step up my game."

ERIK LOOKED AT Emma still tangled in her pajama top, lacy bra parted to reveal her perfect pink-tipped breasts, and felt something weird in his chest.

Yeah, he was hard as a baseball bat for her and had nothing more on his mind than making her scream his name, but still something struck him. As if the moment was somehow more than what it was.

So strange.

He pushed her back when she tried to rise again. "Later, okay. Right now, I need to taste you."

Lowering himself, he settled deeper under the covers. He slipped his hands beneath her perfect ass and pushed her up toward the creaking headboard. "Are you too cold?"

She shook her head, pretty emerald eyes wide and

riveted to him. He grabbed the abandoned pillow and handed it to her. "Use this."

Then he turned his attention back to that which drew him like steel to a magnet. He kissed a line across her belly, stopping every so often to nip at the lace. Then he nuzzled the plump flesh that covered her pubic bone, allowing the delicate silk to catch on his beard as he moved his face back and forth, inhaling her unique scent.

He clasped her knees and lifted them, pushing them back so she was more open to him. She still wore the fuzzy socks, which should have looked silly, but there was something erotic in half-dressed Emma spread before him. She squeaked, but her breathing increased and he knew she was turned on. "Hold your knees, baby. I'm going to be too busy to do it myself."

Emma did as she was told, holding her legs back, socked feet planted on the lumpy mattress. She looked like an offering to him.

Which, of course, she was.

Erik nuzzled her through the silk and lace, groaning when the slick damp fabric yielded the taste of her. Nothing turned a man on more than knowing how wet a woman was for him. Carefully, he used his finger to slide beneath the crotch, stroking the outside fold that was slick and oh-so perfect.

Emma moaned and her head hit the iron of the bed, but she didn't release her knees. And a second later, he felt her watching him as he licked her through her panties.

Another turn-on. He loved when a girl watched him go down on her.

Slowly he lifted the material, sliding it to one side, revealing what he'd been dying to get to. He'd wanted to make her beg, but he was near to begging himself at the sight and smell of her. He ground his cock against the bed, needing some sensation, some relief.

Then he traced a finger through her slick heat. Heaven.

"Oh, oh…" Emma sighed, her eyes never leaving his as he sucked his finger into his mouth.

It was an erotic move and it made her close her eyes. "Oh, Erik. I want more."

He watched her as he lowered his mouth toward the prize. Her mouth fell open as she panted and her eyes dilated. He paused right over the tight rosy bud he knew ached for him. And he blew on it.

"Oh, Erik. Oh, you have to…oh…"

He blew again, nearly losing it himself. "You know what you have to do."

Her eyes widened. "Please."

"As you wish," he said then closed his mouth over her clit and sucked.

"Ah," she said, thrusting her hips forward, rocking against him.

He let up on the pressure and used his tongue to stroke her. She tasted incredible, like turned-on woman, and it drove him mad. He increased the pressure and speed of his tongue and then he felt her tighten.

Her scream was the most satisfying sound he'd heard in forever. Her body shook, thighs closing around his head as she rode her climax out. He didn't stop the delicious torture. For one thing, he knew she needed more. For another, he was a selfish bastard who couldn't get enough of Miss Emma Rose's thighs locked around his ears, her honeyed treasure belonging only to him. To do with as he wished. He slid a finger inside her, nearly sighing at the sweet clenching heat of her. He crooked his finger, rubbing her G-spot as he returned his mouth to pleasuring her.

Again she tightened, and again she screamed as she came apart again, her body twisting, ass grinding into the sheets covered with faded forget-me-nots. He held her firm, preventing her from twisting away. Dampness had flooded her with her release and he relished the reward of his efforts. So he continued moving his finger inside her, sucking her clit lightly.

She came again.

Finally he felt a tug at his ears. "Stop, Erik. Please. I can't take any more."

He lifted his head, allowing the lace material to fall back into place. "Good?"

Emma fell back onto the pillows. "Oh, shit."

"I'm going to take that as a yes," he said, wiping her slickness from his mouth and sliding up to kiss her. She didn't shy away from the taste of herself, another mark in her favor. He loved a lusty woman, one who didn't pull back from adventure…from getting really down and dirty in bed.

"You wore me out," she said, brushing another kiss against his lips. "But it's time for *you* to beg, Mr. Matheson."

She pushed him back, rising to her knees, her pajama top still on but parted so her breasts teased him. The air was chilly, so her nipples were hard but her body felt warm enough. She kissed him, twining her arms around him, twisting her fingers in his hair. She kissed him in a way he would never have expected Emma to kiss him—hard, passionately and with wild abandon. Everything about her was so giving…so, so damned sexy.

Drawing back, she traced the ridge of his shoulder. "Are you cold?"

He shook his head. "Not after that. You are so gorgeous. Thank you."

She didn't look at him. Instead, she ran her fingers down his chest. "What for?"

"For not letting me talk myself out of this. I've never been so hot for someone before. You're driving me crazy, lady."

"Mmm," she said, leaning forward and flicking his nipple with her tongue before nipping him. He drew back with an inaudible hiss. But then he stilled himself as she dropped tiny kisses down his stomach, ringing his belly button, hooking her fingers in the waistband of his boxers.

Quickly she slid them down and his cock wagged out to greet her.

Wrapping a hand around his length, she looked up at him. "Very nice."

The pressure of her hand was such sweet torture, but her words of approval were an equal turn-on. She moved her hand slowly, teasing him. Then she cupped his balls, giving them a light squeeze. Erik nearly came right then and there.

"And since you had a taste, it's only fair, right?" she asked, but she didn't wait for permission. She bent, thrusting her ass deliciously into the air, and licked the tip of his cock.

"Ah," Erik breathed, reaching immediately for the golden hair that spilled against his thighs. He pulled it to one side so he could watch her mouth work him.

Grasping the shaft, she wrapped her hand around his rigid length and fastened her pretty mouth around the head of his cock. Slowly and confidently, she began to move.

"Oh, sweet mother of..." He couldn't finish his thought. His entire length was consumed by her and she knew what she was doing, giving pressure, lightening it, releasing her fingers to make a circle lubricated with her saliva, which gave a mind-numbing sensation.

Damned if Miss Emma Rose wasn't incredible at giving head.

He could feel his orgasm building, balls tightening.

It was as if she knew and she slowed her machinations, the pressure on his shaft lifting. She pulled her mouth from him and looked up. "Good?"

He nodded because he had no words and he didn't want to ejaculate yet. He wanted to sink inside her. Of course, as close as he was to coming, there wouldn't be much of an effort given.

Emma leaned forward and ran her tongue over the tip again. "You know what you have to say."

He almost laughed. But couldn't. "Please."

"Good boy," she said, taking him into her mouth again, wrapping her hand around his length, resuming the steady rhythm that had him thrusting his hips forward. The sensation built again, harder and stronger, and then he couldn't stop if he tried. He rode the lightning of his orgasm, pumping into her mouth, half horrified at himself, half out of his mind with pleasure.

Emma didn't stop working him, the torturous pleasure went on and on, making chill bumps ripple over his body. With one last grunt, he emptied himself fully.

She lifted her eyes and unwound her hand from his length. With light suction, she pulled her mouth from him and then scrambled off the bed. He collapsed backward onto the pillows, breathing hard, embarrassed that he couldn't control himself.

There was just something about Emma that made him lose all focus. All control. This wasn't supposed to happen, but there was no way he'd ever regret it.

Besides, they had some unfinished business that the box of condoms could help them with.

Emma came back wiping her mouth. He could smell the toothpaste. She paused at the side of the bed. "I don't swallow."

He started laughing. "Holy cow, woman. Get your sexy ass back in this bed."

Emma smiled and climbed into bed. She'd taken off her bra, but left the open pajama shirt on. Snuggling up, she pulled the blankets over them, straightening the tangle of the sheet as she did. Finally, she sank onto his chest. "That was incredible."

"Mmm-hmm," he said, twisting a length of her hair around his fingers. "Never could have imagined just how talented you were with that mouth."

"I'm a woman of many surprises."

He smiled. "Yes, you are."

She yawned.

"You're not planning on sleeping tonight, are you?"

She popped up. "Why? You have something better we can do?"

"Give me ten more minutes and I'll show you," he teased, dropping a kiss on her stubborn chin. Funny how he'd never noticed that before. Such a thrill to learn the reticent Emma was a freakin' wildcat in the sack.

She lifted herself and kissed him. "Only ten minutes?"

"What can I say? You make me feel like a teenager. Short recovery time."

"This is crazy, but I'm so glad it happened. I've wanted you only forever."

Erik's heart leaped. Which was weird. This wasn't about anything other than one night of crazy sex, right? Still, he kept getting these feelings about Emma. She was so familiar, yet a mystery to him. Gorgeous, smart and sexy, Emma was nearly the perfect woman. She didn't fill silence with noise and she was patient. Still, she didn't let anything stand in her way. He had such admiration for her and at the same time he wanted to consume her. "Have you?"

"Ever since I saw you making out with Whitney in the swimming pool."

"Whitney?"

"Kellogg. She was the head cheerleader. Sort of easy."

"Oh, yeah. Had a big set of jugs?"

"That would be the one."

"You saw me and her making out?"

Emma nodded. "Up until that point, I had always thought you were cute. You know, in that benign way teen girls do. But then I watched you in the pool. Oh, I'm not a pervert. I didn't stay long, but I saw enough to make me feel different about you. I wanted your mouth on me, your hands untying my bikini top. It was like a hunger awoke, and I guess it never really faded."

"Wow," he breathed, stroking her face, running a finger over her bottom lip. "I never knew."

"I'm not like Alexis. I don't usually reveal my feelings. I can't believe I'm being this honest with you now. I guess things just feel different."

"I'm so glad you are. This is so strange, but so wonderful. And we're not finished, sweet Emma. There's so much more I want to do to you. I feel spellbound, like I'm not even me. But then I am, and I want you with everything I am."

7

HIS WORDS MADE her heart ache.

I want you with everything I am.

It was the sort of thing every girl wanted to hear from the guy she'd worshipped for years. Oh, sure, she'd had boyfriends and hoped for love with them. Erik seemed unattainable, totally off her radar. Until two days ago.

Then he was on it.

Very much on it.

"Should I fetch the box of Magnums?"

He smiled, pulling her down for another kiss. "I think I'm ready," he murmured against her lips.

"Let's see," she said, sliding her hand down to clasp his stirring cock. "Not quite, but I can do something about that."

"Oh no. You nearly killed me a few minutes ago." He curved an arm around her, pulling her to him, capturing her mouth in a sweet kiss that literally curled her toes that were still in the fluffy polka-dot socks.

He pulled her hand from his crotch. "Let's take this one slow, baby."

Erik rolled her over onto her back, tugging her hip so she slid beneath him. Propped on one elbow, he proceeded to kiss her thoroughly. By the time he'd finished and moved to the sensitive shell of her ear, her pulse galloped and a new achiness had awoken in her pelvis.

She stroked his shoulders, enjoying the feeling of his smooth, strong arms, as she allowed her nails to trail back and forth across the span of flesh. Goose bumps emerged and he moaned with pleasure. Against her leg, his erection grew harder, making sweet heat pool in her belly.

Moving down to her breasts, he lazily loved her, pausing to kiss, suckle and tease.

Finally he lifted himself, shifting over to drag the trunk toward the bed. Cool air rushed in between them, but seconds later, he was back, covering her, warming her. In his hand he held a condom package.

She took it from him and he kissed her once again, his hands stroking the length of her body, pausing to roll a nipple or tease her belly button. Pulling back from him, she used her teeth to rip the package, withdrawing the circular condom. "I can put this on with my mouth," she teased.

He closed his eyes and breathed deeply. "I think you better use your hand if you want this to last."

Giving him a mischievous smile, she placed the condom on the head of his cock and slowly rolled it down his length. He was the perfect size for her. Big and thick, but not porno monstrous. She loved the feel of him in her hand, even with the condom on.

Erik pushed her back and settled himself between her legs, sliding himself back and forth in the slickness of her body. His lips caught hers again and he whispered, "I could fall in love with a woman like you."

He lifted her thighs and tilted his hips before sliding inside her, burying himself to the hilt.

"Oh," she breathed as he filled her. It wasn't just the physical act of taking her, but the words. Again, his honeyed words wrapped round her, sweet nothings whispered in the act of passion. But somehow they seemed to be more. She wanted them to be. She needed them to fill the small box of hope inside her heart.

He began to move, eyes closed.

The sensation was so good, she closed hers, too. She lost herself in the moment, his hands clasping her hips, his breathing ragged in her ear as he dropped tiny kisses sporadically on the shoulder that had slipped out of the pajama top. Emma lifted her knees, hugging his lean hips, and rode with him toward that beautiful pinnacle.

"So...so..." he panted, kissing her jaw before capturing her lips again. "So good."

He increased the tempo and she lifted her bottom so he touched that spot. Inside, she felt the tension build, gathering deep in her pelvis. She surrendered to it, letting it rip through her, washing over her with tingling warmth.

Seconds later, Eric joined her, his guttural cry in her ear as he pumped into her.

Finally, he collapsed atop her, breathing hard, kissing her shoulder, whispering things about how good she was, how tight, how perfect, how sexy. Emma wrapped her arms around him, holding him close to her.

Their hearts beat together as time slowed and the chill around them permeated.

Erik lifted his head and studied her.

"What?" she asked after several seconds.

"I'm amazed by this. Sounds silly but I never planned on feeling so…so…right with you."

"Why not? Because of Alexis?"

Erik swallowed. "Maybe. I don't know. I guess I just never imagined that you were a possibility. I always liked you, but never allowed myself to see you as anything other than what you were to me—a cute friend of my sister's. But you're so much more and it's like stumbling over a winning lottery ticket. Where there once was not much, now there is such possibility."

Emma watched him, wondering what he meant.

She'd said this was supposed to be a one-night thing, a crazy act they'd never discuss again, but maybe he saw there could be something more. She wanted that. Oh, how she wanted that, but she didn't want to be that kind of girl. The kind that said one thing to get what she wanted but changed the game to suit herself later. She'd never press him for any kind of relationship if he saw this only as a hookup.

Erik withdrew from her, reaching down to deal with the spent condom. This time he was the one padding to the bathroom. Seconds later, he returned, handing her a length of the precious toilet paper so she could do cleanup. Afterward, Erik tugged on his socks and T-shirt, handed her the pajama bottoms and pulled her to him. Flipping the blankets back atop them, he sank into the lumpy mattress, settling her beside him.

After a few minutes of contemplating the darkness, Emma asked, "What did you mean by all that?"

"Hmm?"

"That there is 'possibility'?"

"Oh, well…" He hesitated as if he wasn't even sure what he'd meant. "I know we kinda agreed that this would be a one-time thing, but…"

"You want more?" She took the hope out of her voice. She didn't want to sway him, didn't want him to know how much she wanted him to say yes.

"I don't know, Em," he said, kissing her forehead. "I think right now we should enjoy what we have. We can talk about how this will shake out later."

In the light of day.

She knew how that worked. In the intimate darkness of the now-not-so-cozy cabin, what they had was one thing. Come morning, with the bright light creeping in between the gingham curtains and the nearly empty bottle of tequila staring them in the face, it would be quite another. Neither would have to take a walk of shame, but no doubt he'd regret doing his little sister's BFF.

"Go to sleep, baby," he said, kissing her softly.

His words had the intended effect and she closed her eyes and snuggled deeper into his side. Her thoughts were a tangle of possibility, hope, embarrassment, but no shame. She wouldn't change the amazing night she'd had with Erik. Even if the morning brought a painful resolution.

Softly, fatigue crept on her and with the warmth of the man next to her, she began to fall into sleep.

The last thought she had before she checked out was that she didn't think she'd ever come so many times in one night.

ERIK WOKE BEFORE Emma to weak light streaming through the crack of the curtains. The cabin still looked shrouded in darkness and part of him longed to burrow under the covers with Emma, shutting out the world.

But the cabin was ice cold.

Carefully he slipped from beneath her arm and slid out of bed, grabbing the jeans he'd discarded the night before. Quick as a cat, he used the john, brushed his teeth with the extra toothbrush and built a fire, wishing like hell they had some coffee. He puffed into his hands while he waited for the fire to catch and once it had, he hotfooted it back to the bed, shucked off his jeans and climbed in next to Emma.

"Oh," she said when he wrapped his arm around her. "You're so cold."

"Had to start a fire. It's freezing in here, but you're warm as toast, babe," he said, bundling her into his arms.

"Ah, you feel like ice," she squealed, pushing him away.

"Come on, I need your warmth," he said, hauling her against him.

This time she didn't struggle. Instead, she rubbed her hands up and down his arm, trying to warm him. Generous Emma. His heart beat harder in his chest as he thought about her last night.

She'd been spectacular.

He'd been with a lot of women. He wasn't a man whore, but he rarely turned down the company of a beautiful, willing lady. And he couldn't remember ever being so blown away. The sex had been hot as hell. But not only that, they'd had fun together, putting together a puzzle, shooting tequila and teasing one another. Thing was, he genuinely liked being with her, which surprised him. He thought he'd had her pegged as an uppity intellectual, but Emma had an earthy charm, a whimsical sense of humor and a giving nature. She was a dream package of a woman.

"Warmer now?" she asked.

He gathered her in tight to him, resting his chin atop her head. "Perfect."

"I wish I had a cup of coffee." She sighed against his chest.

He laughed. Great minds do think alike. "Can I interest you in half a glass of wine or tequila?"

"Ugh," she groaned.

"Oh, come on. You know what they say about tequila."

"It makes your panties drop?"

"Oh, is that what it is?" he joked, twisting a finger in her hair. "I thought it was something about not remembering things."

"Is that what you wish? Not to remember?" Her voice had grown serious and his remark from last night came back to peck at him. He hadn't meant to suggest they had to follow up their night of kick-ass sex with something more. Hadn't she been the one to suggest that it could be like one of those bizarre encounters both parties blame on the liquor and loneliness? He didn't want to change the rules when she'd been so careful to brand it as a onetime thing.

"No. I will always cherish getting stranded with you in this cabin. And so you know, we're still stranded, so how about—" he slid his hand up her thigh, relishing her flesh even through the soft flannel "—we not waste this fabulous lumpy bed with the broken springs?"

He lowered his head to kiss her.

But her hand stopped him. "I want to brush my teeth first."

"Don't worry. A little morning breath won't hinder me."

"Nope. You brushed yours. Besides, I can still taste the booze." She sat up and gave a little shiver. "Be right back."

Erik flopped back, smiling as he watched her run to the small bathroom off the main room, teeth chattering. He liked her pluck…and that she was thoughtful about hygiene. It took him back to last night and her hopping from the bed after giving him the most excruciatingly wonderful pleasure with her pretty mouth.

In less than a minute she ran back, jumping into bed, her body shaking. "Holy Moses, it's so cold."

"The fire will get us warm…but first let's make our own heat."

Emma giggled.

"What? Too cheesy?"

"Yeah, but I like cheesy sometimes. Come on, big boy. Come light my fire." She curved a hand around his neck and tugged him to her.

"Isn't that a song?" he murmured, dropping kisses on lips that tasted of toothpaste.

"Mmm-hmm," she moaned, opening her mouth to him. He started unbuttoning her pajama top, dying to see her breasts in the faint light of day. In the flickering light of the dying fire, they'd been so perfect, but he needed to see the pink-tipped breasts, taste them once again.

When he reached the last button, he broke the kiss, pulling the covers back so he could see her. It had grown lighter in the past half hour and now the darkness had been replaced by the grayness of dawn.

He had been right. Her breasts were perfect, gently sloped, fuller on bottom than top, the nipples a dusky pink. They were hard for him, begging him to taste them.

So he obliged, softly kissing the one closest to him, sucking her into his mouth.

Emma hissed, her head falling back on the pillow. "Oh, Erik. That's so nice."

"Is it, baby?" he said, turning his attention to the other breast, pressing her back onto the bed.

Emma nodded, her eyes closing as he worshipped the beauty before him. He traced a finger down her belly, which was flat and much smaller at the waist than he remembered. Slowly he slipped a hand into her pajama pants, burrowing beneath her panties to cup her sex. She was slick and ready for him.

He allowed his middle finger to slip inside to the sweet dampness and, finding her clit, he began to make tiny circles.

"Oh," she said, arching her back before thrusting her hips upward.

"Easy, babe," he said, allowing her nipple to slide from his mouth. "I want to watch you come. Will you come for me, Emma?"

"If you keep doing that," she said, opening her eyes to watch him.

At that moment, he knew he needed to see all of her. He slipped his hand from her and lifted himself slightly so he could slide her pajama pants down past her knees. Then he did the same with her panties.

"Oh, sweetheart, you're so pretty," he said, feathering through the trimmed hair covering her. He parted her folds with his fingers, catching a peek of the small bud. He started the circles again, shifting his gaze from her sweet womanhood to the pleasure on her face.

"Oh, heavenly days. Don't stop. Don't you dare stop," she groaned.

"Not even if a herd of buffalo stampeded," he said, quickening his movements, pausing only to move down, slipping his finger inside her before returning to her clit again. He loved the feel of her—so warm, wet and womanly. It was addictive.

Emma moved her hips, her eyes screwed closed as her breath came in short pants. Then suddenly her entire body tightened.

"Ah," she moaned, her hands slamming down to clutch the sheets as she rode her orgasm.

He didn't let up. Watching her come was also addictive and he wanted to see it again. And again. And again. Making love to Emma was one of the best things he'd done in forever. He wanted to savor the sight of her coming undone, the smell of their passion, the feel of her body clenching around him.

"Oh, oh, please," she panted, sliding her hands up to cup her own breasts. That sight refueled him and he slid his finger inside her, moving rhythmically, finding that sweet, sweet spot that would launch her anew.

And it did.

A new round of tightening, legs shaking as she found her release again.

"Don't stop," she yelled, thrusting her hips in time with him, feet planted, mouth open. "What are you doing to me?"

"No, what are you doing to me?" he asked, meaning it. This gorgeous woman was splendidly wrought, made to be played by his hands.

Suddenly she pushed his hand from her body. "I want you. Inside me." She reached for his waistband.

"You don't have to ask twice." He shucked off his boxers and reached for the box of condoms. She tried to take the package from him, but he brushed her hand away. Jabbing on the condom, he rolled it down his length and nudged her legs apart so he could settle into the sweetest place imaginable.

Slowly he inserted the head of his cock, sighing at the tight warmth. He bit his lip, trying to go slow, wanting to savor every inch of pleasure. Emma had other ideas. She clamped her thighs around his hips and lifted her ass, taking him all the way inside her.

"Yes…" She sighed.

He started moving again, so slow it almost hurt.

"No, no," she said, smacking his ass. "Harder, please."

Smiling, he tossed his intentions aside and gave her

what she wanted. Several minutes later he found his own release.

Their breaths and cries of pleasure twisted together in the oldest song known to man.

And it was so good.

8

THE LIGHT OF morning had not brought regrets. On the contrary, it had brought more of the fantasy Emma had wrapped herself in. She wasn't tugging it off until she had to.

She lay twined in Erik's arms, totally sated. "That was nice."

"Nice? Don't you mean spectacular?"

She gave him a little pinch. "You think highly of your abilities, don't you?"

He looked at her and crooked an eyebrow, making her laugh.

"Okay, okay, I can honestly say it was spectacular," she said, giving him a kiss.

Just as she was breaking the kiss, the front door slammed open, breaking the chair, sending it careening across the worn floor.

She screamed, clutching the covers to her. Erik jumped out of bed and grabbed the lamp he'd set beside the trunk, raising it like a weapon. At first she thought the wind had gusted hard enough to once again blow the door open. But then she saw the man…and the gun.

"Get your hands up," the intruder yelled, stepping into the cabin holding a shotgun.

She didn't want to put her hands up. If she did, her boobs would be out there for all to see. Tucking the covers under her arms, she pressed her upper arms to her sides and held up her hands. Erik dropped the lamp and the ceramic base shattered on the floor.

A large man wearing a brown cowboy hat and a fluffy khaki ski jacket with a star attached strolled in. Removing his mirrored glasses, he made a face. "Just what in the hell is going on here? You know you're trespassing, don't you?"

Erik kept his hands up. "We had an accident up on the highway yesterday and we couldn't find help."

"So you broke into my cabin?" an older man asked, stepping forward.

"Well, our car was dead and neither of our cell phones worked," Erik said, gingerly lowering his arms while eyeing the shotgun still pointed at them. "We stayed on the highway for a long time, but no one came. We saw the reflective marker on the highway and found this place."

"We'll pay for repairs to the door," Emma added, sliding her eyes to the shattered lamp. "And the lamp."

The deputy turned to the older man, who had a bristly mustache and wore hunting coveralls. "You gonna press charges, Walt?"

Walt looked at Erik and then looked at her. A knowing gleam appeared in his eyes. "Ah, hell. I can't press charges against people taking shelter from the storm.

Gave us nearly a foot last night. Besides it's Christmas and all."

"Thank you," Emma said, looking over to Erik, who looked like a man with his hand caught in a cookie jar. Yeah, her cookie jar.

"We would appreciate that, sir," he said finally.

"Ah, hell, this place ain't been used in years," Walt said, stepping in and closing the door. "No electricity or anything. If you'd have come a quarter mile more, you would have hit my spread. This here was my groundskeeper's place back when I needed someone. Sold most my land but kept this old cabin. My boys always liked to have friends over to play cards, drink hooch and blow up stuff. So don't worry about the lamp. No loss there."

The deputy looked around and then resettled his gaze on them. "Why don't we let these two get decent and then I'll run them up to your house so they can call a tow truck."

Walt nodded. "Yeah, come on up to the house and I'll get you some coffee and a proper breakfast. Maria made enough muffins for Cox's army. I'll wait outside."

The deputy followed Walt out, closing the broken door.

Her heart raced and she felt sweaty despite the new chill in the air.

"You okay?" Erik asked, reaching for his jeans and pulling them on. The tender teasing was gone, replaced by something she couldn't put her finger on. Probably that whole light-of-day thing. Or the sober realization they'd stepped over a line they couldn't backtrack over. Or maybe it was just having a shotgun trained on him.

"I'm fine," she said, suddenly feeling shy about her nudity. Minutes before, she'd been crying his name, shattering in his arms. But now it felt sordid. She'd seen the look in those men's eyes. They knew what had gone down in the cabin last night. And it damn sure wasn't completing a puzzle.

"At least we don't have to go up to the highway and look for help. It came to us."

"Yeah," she agreed, reaching for the pajama top she'd shed earlier. She didn't want to bare her breasts. Silly, of course, but she felt so vulnerable. In the blink of an eye, Erik had gone from tender lover to a man ready to stride back into his regular world. "Guess I better go get my things out of the bathroom."

"The water in the pot should be warm enough to wash up a bit. I'll put it in the bathroom," he said, tugging on the sweater he'd left by the fire before lifting the pot.

Emma couldn't help it. She blushed. If anyone needed cleaning up, it was her. They'd had sex three— or was it four?—times. She needed a good long soak, but lukewarm water dipped from a pot would have to do.

She scrambled from the bed and five minutes later emerged from the bathroom with her hair braided, face scrubbed clean and lip gloss firmly in place. She pulled on her ruined boots and shrugged into her wool coat. "I'm ready."

Erik had donned his coat and scarf and had moved everything back into its original order. He'd bundled the sheets into a ball, which he carried out with them. Walt and the deputy sat in a cruiser emblazoned with the Douglas County Sheriff's Office on the side. Erik held the back door for her and then set her suitcase between them, holding sheets that were the last reminder of their wild winter night.

"I brought the sheets. Figured they'd need to be washed," Erik said to Walt.

"Sure. My housekeeper, Maria, will wash them and I'll run them back later. Probably should clean that place up a little anyway. Maybe stick some rations in there in case another couple gets stranded again. Probably would have been nice to have some food."

"We survived on wine and chocolate-chip cookies," Erik said.

"Don't sound bad at all," the deputy said, backing around and turning toward the highway. "You folks were lucky to find shelter. A man died last year in the same situation. He stayed in his wrecked car and died of carbon monoxide poisoning. The snow clogged the tailpipe."

Fifteen minutes later, Emma was seated in the kitchen of Walt's enormous house, sipping a cup of coffee and trying not to wolf down the fluffy blueberry muffins Maria had set in front of her and Erik. Christmas music played in the kitchen and a pretty flocked tree glittered in the living area opened to the kitchen. Quite the opposite of the dusty cold cabin they'd abandoned moments ago.

Still, Emma longed for the cabin and the sweet love that had bloomed there if only for a night. Nothing seemed to remain of what they'd shared. Erik had withdrawn, passing over the sheets and blankets to Maria, erasing any evidence of their lovemaking. Or maybe she read too much into how easily he went back to normal. She didn't feel normal. More like confused and scared of all the feelings she'd unearthed for Erik.

He glanced at her. "You okay? You're awfully quiet."

"Sure." What else could she say? That she already mourned the loss of him. That her heart already felt wounded. Maybe actually broken. But that was crazy, right?

"I called a tow-truck company and they're supposed to get back to me on when they can make it down here. Deputy Shane said he'd write out a report. Here's his card for when you call your insurance company." He handed her the card.

"Thank you. I called my parents while you were on the phone. They flipped out but they're glad I'm safe."

"More muffins?" Maria interrupted with a gap-toothed smile. She filled Erik's mug and arched a brow.

"You bet," he said with a nod of thanks. "Good as my grandmother's and that's saying something."

Maria giggled and waddled back to the stove.

"I don't think Alexis ever got your text," Erik said, munching on the muffin Maria brought over. "I tried calling but her phone is off."

Walt toddled in. "Bad news. Roads aren't passable yet. Called the sheriff and he said he'd call the county to send the snowplows out. You're probably going to have to stay here tonight. Got plenty of room and we're stocked, right, Maria?"

"*Sí*, Señor Grider, and I'm preparing a wonderful dinner tonight for your guests," she said.

"We don't want to be a bother," Emma said, feeling

disappointed though she knew she should be grateful they were warm and safe.

"You no bother," Maria said, swatting a hand at them. "Señor Grider loves having company. And his boys are not coming till Tuesday, *si*?"

Walt nodded.

Erik looked at her. "At least we'll have hot water."

"And something more than cookies and chocolate for dinner."

"Yeah, but I liked having dessert first," Erik said.

ERIK STEPPED FROM the shower, drying the rivulets streaming down his face. He glanced at himself in the mirror and noted his beard had gotten way too thick. He looked like a wild mountain man and, after the night he'd spent with Emma, he felt like one.

She'd asked for her own room and that told him all he needed to know.

Maybe she'd just needed some space.

But the way she'd looked at him, the way she'd shut down, worried him. He'd tried to tease her with the whole dessert-first thing. That's how he felt about them. As though maybe they'd had dessert first when they'd indulged in each other at the cabin, but he hoped they could use their lovemaking as a starting point for something more.

Wrapping the plush towel around himself, he walked into the bedroom. Folded neatly on the bed was a pair of jeans and Henley shirt. A new package of boxers and a neatly folded pair of socks sat on the end of the bed, convincing him Walt likely had sons the same size. In the bathroom, he found enough toiletries to make himself presentable. Glancing at his watch, he saw it was only ten o'clock in the morning, but he felt bone weary. Eyeing the bed, he wondered if he should nap…and then he wondered if he could talk Emma into napping with him.

His cell phone vibrated on the rough-hewn dresser.

"Hey, man, there you are," Layton said. "Your sister was freaking out because you didn't call."

"Well, I took a short cut that didn't work out so well. I hit a patch of ice, overcorrected and ended up plowing Emma's car into a tree. We didn't have cell service and had to take shelter in an abandoned cabin overnight. But we're good. All our toes and fingers are still intact." No need to mention exactly how they'd stayed warm.

"All right, that sucks but glad to hear you're okay. That could've ended a lot worse. So you're going to stay there until the car is repaired?"

"Yeah. Won't be able to get a tow truck until tomorrow, but both Emma and I are safe and warm. The owner of the cabin is putting us up for the night," Erik said, oddly glad he still had one night left with Emma…even if she was acting weird. He wasn't ready to go back to his version of reality. "How's my sister?"

His friend hesitated. "Alexis's foot is fine. The swelling went down and we didn't need to take her to the hospital. I've been taking real good care of her."

"Have you now?"

An uncomfortable silence sat for a few seconds.

"Dude, my sister doesn't need what you can give her," Erik said, knowing he overstepped but also knowing his sister and the reputation of his friend with the ladies.

"Don't worry about Alexis… I've got everything under control." Layton's voice lowered.

"You're a good guy, but she's had it tough these last few months. She doesn't need any more heartache. She needs stability and to get her life straight again before jumping into something."

No doubt Layton and Alexis had some little flirtation. His sister could use the ego boost after her last boyfriend had gutted her self-confidence. Which was hard to believe when it came to a woman like his sister.

"Hey, bud, I do appreciate your looking out for Alexis while she is banged up. I wasn't trying to disparage your character. You're a good guy. I'm just a big brother concerned about his sister."

"We'll talk more when you get home," Layton said. "Drive safe."

Erik hung up and sank onto the bed. The whole Alexis-Layton thing bothered him. But to a degree, his friend was right. There was only so much he could do. His sister had to live her own life, and he had to live his.

Thing was, he wanted to live his life seeing his sister's best friend.

Emma Rose had knocked him for a loop. Never could he have imagined how incredible the woman behind the image he'd painted in his mind could be. He'd loved being with her, loved her teasing, the way she launched herself into any task, the way she listened to him, respected him…loved him.

Okay, he couldn't be so presumptuous, but damned if there wasn't something strong…and magical between them.

Weird to think of it as some fated thing, but that's what it felt like. It was as if everything that had happened was preordained, designed for him in the stars. He'd never been the kind of guy to need a relationship, but something about Emma made him want more. Maybe he was going bonkers. But he didn't think so. Because beneath his tough-guy exterior beat a heart longing for something more…and he was almost certain that Emma was part of it.

But she'd withdrawn from him both physically and mentally.

How could he reach her and show her he wanted more?

9

EMMA FINISHED DRYING her hair and slipped into the dress and tights she'd planned to wear to her parents' party last night. It was a bit fancy for dinner at Walt's house, but she didn't have anything beyond a long-sleeved T-shirt and jeans. The clothes she'd worn yesterday held too many memories for her to handle… along with the fact she'd torn a hole in the knee of her leggings.

After gulping down the coffee and muffins, she'd requested a room and had been so exhausted she'd conked out on the bed without even taking off her boots. She'd slept for four hours, waking stiff and sore from her adventure, both inside and outside the cabin. Groggy, she'd run a bath and lay in the bubbles for another half hour. After washing her hair and scrubbing her body with a lovely lavender herbal soap, she felt almost human again.

At least on the outside.

Inside, her mind kept tripping back to Erik's reaction

to their being discovered. He'd been so unaffected…
so normal.

Like nothing had happened.

And that hurt.

Last night she'd implied she could handle whatever
happened between them, but she couldn't. Wasn't as if
she'd lied—she wanted to be the girl who could sleep
with a guy without dreaming about their babies. She ad-
mired modern women who could love 'em and leave 'em,
but she wasn't wired that way. Never had been. And even
if she was, her problem was she'd already been half in
love with Erik before she'd slept with him.

So where did that leave her?

She'd sensed Erik's surprise when she requested
her own room, but she didn't feel comfortable sleeping with him at the moment. Not when they were back
in the real world. And Walt arching a questioning look
at them at her request only made her feel worse. He
didn't know they weren't a real-life couple. So why not
continue the facade for another night?

Didn't she want to spend more time wrapped in
Erik's arms?

Shaking her head, answers escaping her, she swiped
on her lip gloss and opened the door. Walt's house was
like none she'd ever seen. The rancher obviously took
great pride in his Colorado mansion, sprawling against
the evergreen landscape. A small creek ran through
the vaulted foyer built of solid stone. Everything was
wrought by a master craftsman and the effect was stunning. She found Erik and Walt in the vast great room.
A fire roared in the massive stone fireplace, a huge

Christmas tree glittered and the two men looked relaxed, sipping liquor out of highball glasses.

Walt stood. "Well, now, don't you look pretty as a tulip."

"Thank you," Emma said, ducking her head, before remembering she wasn't supposed to be the old Emma. Lifting her chin, she smiled. "How are you gentlemen this afternoon?"

"Well, thank you," Walt said, extending a hand toward the built-in bar. "Pick your poison, madam."

Erik rose and met her at the bar. "I'll fix you something."

"I can do it myself."

"Well, hell, since you're over there, Matheson, fix me another double. Maria will bring in some hors d'oeuvres in a few," said Walt, clearly oblivious to the tension.

Erik touched her hand, making her stomach tremble nervously. She wanted to let go of her fears, but the uncertainty between them kept her guarded.

"You okay?" he asked.

"You keep asking me that," she said, grabbing a glass and pouring a measure of what looked to be small-batch bourbon. She wasn't much of a bourbon drinker but she needed something to calm her. "I'm fine."

"We need to talk."

Emma nodded. "But later. Mr. Grider has been so kind to us, it would be rude to excuse ourselves now. After dinner."

He nodded and she took a sip, restraining herself

from crinkling her nose at the strength of the whiskey. "Tell us about yourself, Mr. Grider."

"Honey, call me Walt," the older man said, a twinkle in his eye. "I do love having a pretty woman to dine with me. I'm tempted to throw this one out in the snow and keep you for myself, but I'm thinkin' I'd have a fight on my hands."

Erik nodded. "That you would."

"I gather you're not originally from Colorado?" Emma asked, settling in a gorgeous chair straight out of *Architectural Digest*.

"Heard my Georgia accent, huh?" Walt teased, before launching into the tale of a Southern boy falling in love with the mountains.

Hours later after a dinner that Emma could only describe as one of the best of her life, they retired to the great room to enjoy after-dinner drinks. After another hour of chitchat, Erik looked at Emma. "Mr. Grider— Walt—I hope you won't mind if I steal Emma away for a moment?"

The older man stroked his mustache. "Can't say I haven't enjoyed the company, but I'm an old man who firmly embraces early to bed, early to rise. I'll say good-night now."

Emma and Erik both said their good-nights, reiterating their gratitude for his hospitality.

After Walt had left, Erik turned to her. "Have I done something wrong?"

She shook her head. "No. I suppose I'm a little freaked out by…everything."

"Do you regret what happened?"

Emma wanted to pace. She felt so unsettled, like

a caged leopard. She forced herself to sit. "I said I wouldn't and I mean that. I'm merely having some issues reintegrating myself in reality."

He came to her and brushed a hand across her jaw. "I don't want you to think I'll be any different than I was before."

Her heart leaped at his touch and then sank at his words. His declaration was a needle popping her balloon of possibility. She'd hoped he would want to see her again. That they might not be a one-night thing. But rather something more. "I know."

Her voice wobbled. Damn it.

"Hey," he said, lifting her chin. "I want you to be happy."

Unshed tears clogged her throat.

She pressed her fingernails into the palm of her hand and willed herself not to cry. This was why he'd had reservations about making love to her in the first place. He had asked if she could handle it. So no tears. No regrets.

"Me, too," she managed to say.

"Then why do you sound not okay? I'm worried that we ruined everything."

Emma looked up. "How is anything ruined? I know the score. I get it."

Erik studied her. "What do you get?"

"That it's over. I told you I could do this and I am. It's just—" she swallowed and averted her gaze from his brilliant blue eyes "—harder than I thought."

He tugged her to her feet. "Emma, what are you talking about?"

"I'm talking about me being an idiot. I knew the

way I felt about you would make this difficult. I should have been able to sleep with you and it not be a big deal, but—"

His kiss cut her off.

And it was a sweet, sweet kiss. One hand rose to cup her face, the other gripped her waist, bringing her fully against him. After a few seconds, he drew back and studied her. "I told you that I liked dessert first, remember?"

Emma squinted at him. "Dessert?"

"What we had back at the cabin was like having dessert first, you know? But I want the main course… and the appetizer—" he dropped his head and nuzzled her neck "—and the salad."

"You mean…you want to see me again?" she asked, hope gathering inside her.

Please say yes. Please.

He lifted his head. "Only if you want the same."

EMMA TILTED HER face up, her lips beckoning, her green eyes shimmering with emotion. "I want that more than anything."

He smiled and dropped another kiss on her lips.

Pulling back, she looked up at him. "But I didn't think you wanted anything more. You were so cold this morning."

Erik didn't know what she was talking about. "Cold? Uh, yeah. We both were."

"No, not physically," she said, regarding him with a puzzled look. "Just the way you acted."

"Like how?"

"Go wash up. Here's the sheets. Call your insurance

company." She crossed her arms over herself. "I felt like you were a different person."

"Well, I couldn't stay naked, whispering sweet words in your ear, babe. There was a man holding a gun on us and I was in my underwear. Makes a man feel a bit shaky."

"It wasn't me?"

"Hell no. I felt a bit out of sorts. Just a natural reaction to our situation. But you? You I haven't stopped wanting since we first got into the car yesterday."

"I feel so stupid. I assumed you were done with me, and I didn't want to press you. Didn't want to be that girl who changed the rules."

He pulled her into his arms. "It's okay. We're both new to this thing between us. I'm relieved you want more than last night with me."

She looked up at him, a tear managing to escape. In her eyes he could see more than possibility. In her eyes he saw a future.

Emma Rose Brent hadn't just grown up.

She'd grown up to be the perfect woman for him.

Erik kissed her and then slapped her behind. "Now, about our sleeping arrangements…are you up for, say, an appetizer?"

Emma nodded, a devilish twinkle in her eye. She opened her mouth, but he knew what she was going to say and pressed a finger against her lips.

"Don't even joke about main courses and bringing the beef." He laughed, wrapping her in his arms.

"How did you know?"

"Because dirty minds think alike," he said, sweeping her off the ground and into his arms. He headed toward the guest suites. "And that tells me all I need to know."

She wrapped her arms around him. "What?"

"That you're the perfect girl to spend Christmas with...you're the perfect girl to fall in love with."

* * * * *

COMING NEXT MONTH FROM

Available November 17, 2015

#871 A COWBOY UNDER THE MISTLETOE
Thunder Mountain Brotherhood
by Vicki Lewis Thompson
Whitney Jones and Ty Slater are about to give in to red-hot temptation. When she can't get home for the holidays, at least she can make it to the sexy cowboy's bed...and into his heart.

#872 A TASTE OF PARADISE
Unrated!
by Leslie Kelly and Shana Gray
2 stories in 1! Warm beaches, cool waves and hot, hot nights— turn up the heat with two scorchingly sexy vacation romances!

#873 TRIPLE DARE
The Art of Seduction
by Regina Kyle
Firefighter Cade Hardesty has never been a one-woman man. His whirlwind affair with photographer Ivy Nelson is hotter than a four-alarm blaze—but can he convince her there's more to it than just sparks?

#874 COWBOY PROUD
Wild Western Heat
by Kelli Ireland
Cade Covington hires PR whiz Emmaline Graystone to promote his new dude ranch. But she can't help her lust for the proud rancher—and keeping things professional is one campaign she might lose.

YOU CAN FIND MORE INFORMATION ON UPCOMING HARLEQUIN® TITLES, FREE EXCERPTS AND MORE AT WWW.HARLEQUIN.COM.

HBCNM1115

REQUEST YOUR FREE BOOKS!
2 FREE NOVELS PLUS 2 FREE GIFTS!

HARLEQUIN®

Blaze®

red-hot reads!

YES! Please send me 2 FREE Harlequin® Blaze® novels and my 2 FREE gifts (gifts are worth about $10). After receiving them, if I don't wish to receive any more books, I can return the shipping statement marked "cancel." If I don't cancel, I will receive 4 brand-new novels every month and be billed just $4.74 per book in the U.S. or $5.21 per book in Canada. That's a savings of at least 14% off the cover price. It's quite a bargain. Shipping and handling is just 50¢ per book in the U.S. and 75¢ per book in Canada.* I understand that accepting the 2 free books and gifts places me under no obligation to buy anything. I can always return a shipment and cancel at any time. Even if I never buy another book, the two free books and gifts are mine to keep forever.

150/350 HDN GH2D

Name	(PLEASE PRINT)	
Address		Apt. #
City	State/Prov.	Zip/Postal Code

Signature (if under 18, a parent or guardian must sign)

Mail to the Reader Service:
IN U.S.A.: P.O. Box 1867, Buffalo, NY 14240-1867
IN CANADA: P.O. Box 609, Fort Erie, Ontario L2A 5X3

Want to try two free books from another line?
Call 1-800-873-8635 or visit www.ReaderService.com.

* Terms and prices subject to change without notice. Prices do not include applicable taxes. Sales tax applicable in N.Y. Canadian residents will be charged applicable taxes. Offer not valid in Quebec. This offer is limited to one order per household. Not valid for current subscribers to Harlequin Blaze books. All orders subject to credit approval. Credit or debit balances in a customer's account(s) may be offset by any other outstanding balance owed by or to the customer. Please allow 4 to 6 weeks for delivery. Offer available while quantities last.

Your Privacy—The Reader Service is committed to protecting your privacy. Our Privacy Policy is available online at www.ReaderService.com or upon request from the Reader Service.

We make a portion of our mailing list available to reputable third parties that offer products we believe may interest you. If you prefer that we not exchange your name with third parties, or if you wish to clarify or modify your communication preferences, please visit us at www.ReaderService.com/consumerschoice or write to us at Reader Service Preference Service, P.O. Box 9062, Buffalo, NY 14240-9062. Include your complete name and address.

HB15

They traded the bunched cord back and forth, winding
the lights around the branches until Ty looped the end at
the top. Then they both stepped back and squinted at the
lit Christmas tree to check placement.

"It's almost perfect," Whitney said. "But there's a
blank space in the middle."

"I see it." He stepped forward and adjusted one strand
lower. Then he backed up. "I think that does it."

"I think so, too."

He heard something in her voice, something soft and
yielding that made his heart beat faster. He glanced over
at her. She was staring right back at him, her eyes dark
and her breathing shallow. If any woman had ever looked
more ready to be kissed, he'd eat his hat.

And damned if he could resist her. His gaze locked with
hers and his body tightened as he stepped closer. Slowly
he combed his fingers through hair that felt as silky as he'd
imagined. "We haven't finished with the tree."

"I know." Her voice was husky. "And there's the dancing afterward…"

"We were never going to do that." He pressed his fingertips into her scalp and tilted her head back. "But I think we were always going to do this." And he lowered his head.

She awaited him with lips parted. After the first gentle pressure against her velvet mouth, he sank deeper with a groan of pleasure. So sweet, so damned perfect. She tasted like wine, better than wine, better than anything he could name.

The slide of her arms around his waist sent heat shooting through his veins. As she nestled against him, he took full command of the kiss, swallowing her moan as he thrust his tongue into her mouth.

She welcomed him, slackening her jaw and inviting him to explore. He caught fire, shifting his angle and making love to her mouth until they were both breathing hard and molded together. As he'd known, they fit exactly.

The red haze of lust threatened to wipe out his good intentions, but he caught himself before he slid his hands under her sweater. Gulping for air, he released her and stepped back. Looking into eyes filled with the same need pounding through him nearly had him reaching for her again. "Let's… Maybe we should…back off for a bit."

Don't miss
A COWBOY UNDER THE MISTLETOE
by Vicki Lewis Thompson.
Available in December 2015 wherever
Harlequin® Blaze® books and ebooks are sold.

www.Harlequin.com

Love the Harlequin book
you just read?

Your opinion matters.

Review this book on your favorite
book site, review site, blog or your own
social media properties and share
your opinion with other readers!

THE WORLD IS BETTER WITH

Romance

Harlequin has everything from contemporary, passionate and heartwarming to suspenseful and inspirational stories.

Whatever your mood, we have a romance just for you!

Connect with us to find your next great read, special offers and more.

f /HarlequinBooks

🐦 @HarlequinBooks

www.HarlequinBlog.com

www.Harlequin.com/Newsletters

⬥ HARLEQUIN®

A *Romance* FOR EVERY MOOD™

www.Harlequin.com